BILL RILEY'S HEAD

BILL RILEY'S HEAD

DOUGLAS HIRT

FIVE STAR

A part of Gale, a Cengage Company

GALE
A Cengage Company

Farmington Hills, Mich • San Francisco • New York • Waterville, Maine
Meriden, Conn • Mason, Ohio • Chicago

LIBRARY OF CONGRESS CATALOGING-IN-PUBLICATION DATA

Names: Hirt, Douglas, author.
Title: Bill Riley's head / Douglas Hirt.
Description: First edition. | Waterville, Maine : Five Star Publishing, a part of
    Cengage Learning, Inc., [2017]
Identifiers: LCCN 2017022961 (print) | LCCN 2017027008 (ebook) | ISBN
    9781432838041 (ebook) | ISBN 1432838040 (ebook) | ISBN 9781432838034
    (ebook) | ISBN 1432838032 (ebook) | ISBN 9781432838171 (hardcover) | ISBN
    1432838172 (hardcover)
Subjects: | GSAFD: Western stories.
Classification: LCC PS3558.I727 (ebook) | LCC PS3558.I727 B55 2017 (print) |
    DDC 813/.54—dc23
LC record available at https://lccn.loc.gov/2017022961

First Edition. First Printing: December 2017
Find us on Facebook–https://www.facebook.com/FiveStarCengage
Visit our website–http://www.gale.cengage.com/fivestar/
Contact Five Star™ Publishing at FiveStar@cengage.com

Printed in the United States of America
1 2 3 4 5 6 7 21 20 19 18 17

For David and Alison Sherrow

CHAPTER 1

Whenever I started talking to Blue Shanks like she was a real person, I knew I'd been out hunting too long. Well, she was the only female near enough to talk to at the moment, but soon there would be another. A vision of Francine's lovely face lighted comfortably in my brain, and for a little while I forgot the cloud of stink that hung about me, stuffing up my sinuses.

The breeze shifted, and the gagging stench that had dogged me halfway across the Dakota Territory suddenly wasn't so sharp. Leastwise, its bite became tolerable. Blue Shanks settled down some, too, not fighting the bit so hard. The reprieve could only be temporary as my fight wasn't with the wind; it was with the clock, and where time challenged a man crossing the Dakota Territory a-horseback, the clock usually won. It wouldn't be many more days before . . .

We'd been climbing a long, brittle-grass hill for the last few minutes. Cresting the top now, a glorious sight spread out below.

The Missouri River—wide, snaking, muddy, ripped apart here and there by long, finger-like bars. She'd been a long time coming, and I sat there admiring her and thinking that here was a solution to my problem.

A grin cracked my sun-hardened face. "She's ugly, all right. Everything they claim her to be, but to these eyes, Miss Shanks, that there river is about as purty as a magnolia flower."

I stood in my stirrups to stretch the kinks from my spine and settled back on the seat, the butt of my Remington revolver poking my back ribs in a reassuring manner.

My view shifted from the broad, brown water to the shabby, gray hamlet nestled into one of her wide bends. I had no map to guide by, only the compass of the sun and moon pointing me eastward. Even if I had a map, I doubt it would have marked the names of every shabby town that springs up along the river. Most of these burgs last only a season or three until the river tires of their presence and washes them away.

It appeared that at one time a goodly amount of timber had crowded the riverbank thereabouts, but those trees were long gone, the landscape hacked clean of 'em a couple miles in either direction.

Just then the wind changed direction again. My nose scrunched, and my lips puckered. Blue Shanks shifted under her saddle and tossed her head, too.

"Yes, ma'am. I do agree. This stink is getting mighty ripe." I clucked her forward at an easy trot. The burlap sack tied to the saddle horn bouncing annoyingly against my left thigh, reminding me that time was getting short.

"It won't be long now, old gal." I grimaced as we made for the distant river town. Yes indeed, I'd been out hunting too long when I started talking to Blue Shanks like she was a real person.

The dry prairie grass just sort of petered out and became a rutted track through town. The main road had no name that I could see, nor had any sign announced a name of the town or a population. There seemed to be a goodly number of Injuns about.

Looking around at the buildings perched along the sloping bank of the river, I figured this burg was one heavy snow melt away from a good scrubbing. It was the sort of here-today-gone-tomorrow town that springs up of a sudden and then withers away nearly as suddenly. From appearances, I judged the major industry here had been cutting timber, and, judging by the scant number of trees left, her days were running out.

A cross road staggered down a short hill toward the river and a broad wharf where two piers stretched far out into the lazy water. Maybe a half-dozen buildings staggered down along with it. The raised sidewalk bespoke of deep winter snow and gumbo mud come spring rains. The thought of that made me squirm a little and reminded me why I'd fled the frontier a couple of years ago. Unfortunately Francine's father had a high opinion of money, and Francine, too, liked the niceties city life offered. Civilized living cost money, and when money got short, I just naturally fell back on the only trade I knew. Hunting.

The few folks lingering along the sidewalk generally paid me no attention, except when a gust of wind sent my calling card wafting through the air. Then heads turned my way, mostly out of curiosity. I just grinned back at them and played innocent.

The population seemed divided between whites and Injuns. I couldn't decide which held the majority. On the whole, the place was unremarkable; the shops along the main street were about what you'd find in most frontier towns. On one corner stood the Buffalo Wallow Saloon. Well, every town had at least one. I rode past a general mercantile, a millinery, a café, a greengrocers, a tiny bank wedged between a bakery and Chinese laundry, and a tobacco shop with a carved Injun out front holding a bunch of wooden cigars in his wooden fingers.

Farther on, a second unnamed street dipped steeply toward the river. A little way down it a simple church sat on a stacked-stone foundation. From its tin roof a crude spire reached halfheartedly toward heaven. The church looked to be slowly losing its fight with gravity. Farther down the way a livery sprawled across both sides of the street with corrals and stables. At the very end a sawmill perched atop pilings stood knee deep in the river. A logjam of trees bunched together with chains awaited the sharp teeth of a circular blade. The chugging of a steam engine and the whine of wood being sawn drifted up to me.

When the floods come, that mill will be the first to go.

I peered ahead, past a two-story hardware store and some small buildings that looked to be private homes. Beyond them the road just sort of petered out again like it had begun, becoming a pair of ruts cutting south through the tall grass.

Well, I had no need to go any farther and reined Blue Shanks about, pointing her nose back the way we'd come. To my left was a deputy US territorial marshal's office with the name *B. Bulger* in blue letters on a shingle above the door. The sign looked newly painted.

Past the Buffalo Wallow Saloon I turned down the road toward the river. We passed two alleyways and a row of shops bravely trying to stand up straight on the slanted road. The last of them was an enterprise called Hagmann's Fishworks. Unlike the others, this building stood high on stork-leg stilts as if daring the river to come and test it. I grinned. The man who built it understood the ways of Old Scratch Missouri.

The road ended at a broad wharf I'd spied earlier. Two long piers pushed out into the slow, brown water. An old keelboat was moored to one of them. A little farther down, a Mackinaw pulled at its hawser in the current, its cargo wrapped in dirty, beige canvas covers.

A few men lingered along the wharf, some moving crates, others just hanging about. No one paid me any attention, nor did anyone seem to notice the foul cloud that hovered about me and Blue Shanks like a swarm of black flies. That was likely due to the strong odor issuing from the fish works, a large salting operation by the looks of it. A dozen or so sealed barrels weeping a salt rime through their staves had been stacked near the northern-most pier. Stenciled names like *Fort Sully, Nebraska*

City, City of Kansas, St. Charles indicated their destinations.

I tied Blue Shanks to a rail and dismounted, stretching my back, then unslung the burlap sack from the saddle horn and carried it with me into a ship chandler's shop. The place was dim and smelled of tar. The floorboards creaked. Rows of shelves displayed hanks of chains, yards of sailcloth, gaffs, cables, and tackle of every configuration. Coils of tarred rope and barrels of pitch lent an industrial smell to the place. I didn't feel quite so conspicuous.

"Hello? Anybody here?" No one seemed to be in the place. The closed-in heat settled over me like a wet blanket. Flies buzzed about my ears and crawled into my eyes. I called one last time and made for the door.

Outside, the river breeze carried the smell of fresh-sawn timber. Farther down the wharf a couple workers were busily hauling new-sawn boards from the sawmill to a storage yard, where they stacked them to dry. A two-mule dray was taking on a load of lumber. Nearby, cords of firewood stood in mounds at the edge of the wharf.

Hoping for some information on steamboat schedules, I started for the sawmill, passing a large warehouse with a tiny corral alongside it. A woebegone looking mule stood hipshot, favoring one of its hooves. The hoof, I noted, had a deep split and needed to be trimmed. The mule, like the rest of the town, was in a sad shape. A sign in the warehouse's window stopped me.

Passage up the river and down.
Inquire within.

I stepped through the open door and stood a moment to let my eyes adjust to the cavernous building. Crates and barrels, racks of steel drill pipe, farm implements, and even an immense paddle wheel off a steamboat slowly emerged from the shadows.

11

To my left a counter stretched along one wall. From that direction came a steady *thump . . . thump . . . thump*. A clerk behind the counter was swinging something up and down.

I drifted on over to the counter and startled the man when, by chance, he looked up. The rubber stamp he'd been pounding stopped mid-air. "Didn't hear you come in." He was a husky man with a big, wiry beard, black as coal. Small round spectacles magnified the dark eyes behind them. He appeared perturbed at the interruption and slammed the stamp down on a ticket stub and set it aside, glancing sideways out a dingy window at the pier as if looking for something. He looked back. "Can I help you?"

The name placard on the counter said *Irwin Wert*. I nodded at it. "You Mr. Wert?"

"I am," he allowed, a note of caution in his voice.

"The sign out front says to come in here for passage down river," I said. I'd been three months alone—well, except for Blue Shanks—and it felt good talking to something that could talk back.

He relaxed a bit. "Ah. Of course. I thought maybe you'd just tied up." His quick smile was a grimace that showed more gum than teeth. It didn't look particularly friendly. "Where you heading and when?"

"Fort Leavenworth. I'd leave right now if it can be arranged."

Mr. Wert peered sternly through the thick lenses of his spectacles and then frowned and sniffed the air, looking around.

I sniffed a couple times, looking over my shoulder at the far wall. "Hagmann's Fishworks," I said, pretending to have just noticed the smell, too, as I quietly lowered the sack to the floor and slid it to one side with my boot.

Mr. Wert scowled. "Wonder what sort of fish Hagmann's pickling today."

"No telling," I said with the innocence of a man who'd just

12

passed gas in a crowded hotel lobby and was anxious to divert the blame.

The clerk pulled a ledger book from a slot and flipped through the pages. "Well, sir, I ain't got no steamer scheduled due *right now* or any time soon." He ran a finger down a column of names and mumbled as if to himself, "It'd make little difference if I did, seeing as boat traffic hereabouts is unreliable." He looked up and showed his gums again. "Snags and bars, you know, and sometimes the Cheyenne."

A twinge of worry pinched my chest. Fort Leavenworth by steamer might take all of two to three days. Overland, it'd be at least another two weeks. "You sure? I'm in kind of a hurry."

"Too bad you weren't here yesterday. The steamer *Sombart* showed up unexpectedly. Took on six cords of wood and all of Harel and Alice Lemuel's earthly goods. They closed up shop sudden-like. Moving back home to Omaha, you see." He made it sound matter of fact, like an unexpected steamship arrival was a regular occurrence here.

"Really. Does that happen often?"

The man peered up from his ledger book, his eyeballs larger than life behind the spectacles. "People move out of Bend City almost as fast as the Indians move in."

"No. I mean the unexpected steamboat. Aren't there schedules?"

"Unexpected is sort of how they all arrive here in Bend City. They go up river, and they come back down—usually. See here?" He turned the ledger and pointed at a column. "Last month the steamer *Spread Eagle* came through on the fourteenth bound for Fort Rice. Then on the sixteenth the *Meteor* hauled up and loaded eight cords of wood. It was bound for Bismarck." He flipped a page. "See the list?"

It appeared he was right. Boats came and went in a sort of haphazard fashion. I said, "That's mighty inconvenient."

He shrugged. "Steamers head north and south all the time, but there're no regular schedules. Some companies post 'em as a formality, but I don't know why they bother. This river is too unpredictable to accommodate a schedule. A boat might show up tonight, or it might be three or four days before one appears."

"Only three or four days?"

"Usually one or two will show up every week."

My concerns eased. "I can wait three or four days." That was better than the alternative of another two weeks in the saddle.

"Give me your name and where you'll be staying, and I'll send a boy to fetch you soon as one heading down puts in."

"That'll work. The name's Thomas Ragland. I don't know where I'm staying yet. Any suggestions?" I was growing anxious to be on my way, as the odor was getting intense, and the warehouseman was searching with his nose again.

"Wally Mace lets rooms. He's got four of 'em above his hardware store, south end of Bend Avenue. If you're of a mind to save money, you might just spread a bedroll down along the river. Mosquitoes are kind of thick, but the river's low, and you can catch turtles for dinner. Ever eat turtle?"

I shook my head. "I hear the Cheyenne find turtles tasty, but personally I try to avoid reptilian fare."

Mr. Wert chuckled. "Well, the Big Muddy Café offers up a tolerable meal. Marshal Bulger eats there, and Bulger is mighty particular about food. That says something, don't you think? It's on the corner of River Street"—he pointed at the far wall—"and Bend Avenue, across from the Buffalo Wallow Saloon."

"Thanks." I grabbed up my sack and hurried toward the daylight beyond the big warehouse doors, anxious to be on my way before I had to start making excuses.

CHAPTER 2

Being naturally of an organized mind, I laid out a plan as I rode slowly up River Street. First things first, and the first order of business was finding a place to sleep tonight. I half considered the warehouseman's low-cost suggestion, but I'd already spent too many nights with a saddle for a pillow. The idea of feathers and cotton sort of had an appeal. Second order of business would be to drop Blue Shanks off at the livery stable I'd spied earlier and see to it she was properly brushed and fed. Afterward I'd feed myself.

I drew rein at the corner of River and Bend and scanned the buildings there. The Big Muddy Café sat directly across from me on the southwest corner. I clucked Blue Shanks forward and turned left on Bend Avenue. The café had a single front window overlooking the boardwalk, and as I rode past I noticed a *For Sale* sign in the lower corner of the window.

The hardware store sat at the far end of town and was the largest building in Bend City, mostly because the hotel part of it appeared to take up the entire second story. It was also one of the few that had fresh paint—white. A pair of windows flanked the door.

I tied Blue Shanks to the rail out front and lifted the sack off the saddle horn. Hitching a leg to the raised plank sidewalk and grabbing the porch post, I hauled myself up from the road. I was reaching for the doorknob when an Injun staggered along the boardwalk toward me and swayed to a stop, putting a hand against the hardware store's wall to steady himself. He wore dirty, leather pants, a grimy, gray vest, and a grease-stained, red shirt. Several layers of cheap glass beads hung around his neck. His long, coarse, black hair hung in twisted knots down his back, and his tattered hat showed more holes in it than my Aunt Millie's colander. He looked me up and down, and I reckon he decided he'd found himself an easy mark.

"Whiskey," he said in pretty good English and extended an open palm. The fellow stunk like he'd pissed on himself.

"Phew." I fanned the air in front of my nose. Between him and the stink of the burlap sack, my nose began to burn. "Have you been rolling in buffalo piss, Chief?"

Maybe he didn't understand that? "Whiskey," he uttered again, blinking sleepily and squinting as though to bring me into focus.

I scooted past him, escaped into the hardware store, and closed the door, drawing in a long breath. Axle grease and pine barrels smelled wonderful compared to whatever brand of toilet water that Injun had been wearing.

"They're everywhere these days," a voice said. "They'll steal you blind if you're not careful."

I turned. A man stood near the window, his lanky frame casting a long shadow across a pyramid of small casks labeled *nails*. His hair was longish and graying, his pointed beard meticulously trimmed. He watched the Injun stagger away and then turned from the window and looked me up and down, his nose wrinkling. He removed a short cigar from his mouth and pointed it at me. "Did that Injun stink come in with you?"

"It must have." Who was I to correct him? He turned back to the pyramid and hefted another cask into place.

"You a stranger?"

I smiled. "I am, in some places. Are you Mr. Mace?"

Suspicion narrowed his eyes. "Who's asking?"

"Someone who needs a room for a couple nights. Mr. Wert, the warehouse clerk down on the wharf, told me you can provide one."

His expression eased. He grinned and blew out a cloud of smoke. "Indeed, indeed. It just so happens I have one room left."

"Only one?" That was a lie, but I didn't call him on it. "Sounds like something that might fetch a premium."

"Supply and demand, the grand pillar of capitalism. Thirty-five cents a night."

"That's pretty steep. Clean sheets?"

"I have the Chinkies down the street launder them every month whether they need it or not."

I'd slept on worse, but I wasn't going to tonight—not without a haggle. "I can afford a quarter a night."

The man gave an indifferent shrug and went back to work on his growing pyramid of nail casks. By the looks of the stack he was building, he must have been expecting a building boom in Bend City.

I gave a long, loud sigh. "Reckon I'll be spreading my bedroll alongside the river tonight," I said and reached for the door.

"I've always been a sucker for hard-luck cases," Mace said, hefting another cask into place. He looked at me. "You said two nights?"

"Maybe three. Depends on the arrival of the next steamer heading downriver."

"All right. Twenty-five a night." Mace crooked a finger for me to follow him. We went past shelves of draw knives and pocket knives, saws and hatchets, through a back door and up a narrow staircase that made a hard turn halfway up and spilled us out into a dark hallway with five doors.

He opened one of them to an eight-by-ten room. Stale air hit me in the face with the heat of a furnace. A single bed stood against the wall, and a lone chair by the closed window. There wasn't a table. Mace tugged at a stubborn window until it opened.

I pulled back the covers to check for bedbugs. The sheet looked clean enough in spite of a rumpled depression in the middle left by the previous occupant. I prodded the pillow with a finger, a small grin moving across my face. Feathers and cotton! No hard leather and hard ground tonight.

"I'll take it."

Mace was sniffing the stagnant air and looking around. "That's not Injun stink." His view circled the room and zeroed in upon the oily burlap sack in my fist. "What do you have in there?"

I feigned surprise, looking at the sack and then back at Mace. "Dinner."

"Dinner my as—" He caught himself. "—my foot."

"No feet. Just some buffalo tongue and cheese."

"Cheese?" His eyes compressed suspiciously. "What kind of cheese smells like dead fish?"

"Limburger."

"You ain't intending to keep that in this room, are you?"

"It's my dinner," I pleaded innocently. I wasn't much fond of lying, but I cared even less for nosy shopkeepers.

Mace stuck his head out the window and felt around on the wall outside. "There's a nail here I use to hang bunting on for the Fourth of July. Hang your dinner outside the window before it fumigates the place."

I understood his concern and nodded agreeably. "I won't be spending much time here anyway."

I paid him a quarter, and we left the room. Mace said, "The downstairs door to the store will be locked when I leave for the day." He pointed to a door at the end of the hallway. "That one goes outside. It's never locked." We left by way of that door and a rickety staircase down the outside of the building. Mace returned to his shop by way of the front door while I swung a leg over Blue Shanks.

My next stop was the livery stable around the corner, just past the leaning church, which according to a sign out front was of the Methodist persuasion.

Blue Shanks and me found ourselves in a large, dark barn filled with the familiar odor of manure and hay. The "stink" that Mr. Mace called "Injun stink" was hardly noticeable at all here. I spied a man in a far stall, bent over with a big trimming file, working the hoof of a tall bay.

"You in charge?" I asked.

He straightened up slowly with a hand pressed to the small of his back and gave a grimace of pain. "That would be me. I'm Toby McGill."

Toby McGill was a short, stout man, with the powerful arms of a farrier. He'd plainly swung an anvil hammer a time or two. I've never yet met a farrier who couldn't out Injun wrestle men twice their size.

"T. J. Ragland. I've been a few months on the trail. Blue Shanks here, she's a trooper. She's needing a clean stall and some grain. Her shoes might need to be reset. I'll be staying above the hardware store a couple days, till the next steamer south shows up."

McGill huffed. "If someone'd give me fifty bucks for this place I'd be right there on that steamer with you, Mr. Ragland." He gave Blue Shanks a professional up and down look, and a brisk rub behind her ears. "You're a handsome mare."

That was the gospel truth, and Blue Shanks knew it. She took to McGill like a politician to graft. I knew she'd be in good hands. I hefted off the gunny sack, slipped out my saddle carbine, and slung my saddlebags over my shoulder.

McGill took her reins and led her toward an empty stall down at the far end of the barn.

"I'll be by later," I called.

McGill lifted an arm to show he'd heard me and went right to work removing her bridle and saddle.

I'd seen to the first two items on my list and planned on finishing up business for today with a big plate of food. I hiked back up to Bend Avenue and turned my steps toward the Big Muddy Café.

The café was mostly deserted. According to a railroad clock on the wall, the time was three thirty-five. The strong odor of frying liver and onions from the stove in back helped hide the stink that followed me inside.

I aimed for a table in a back corner, figuring to distance the stench some from a couple of diners along the counter. I'd grown skittish, I admit. Hadn't been so when it was just me and Blue Shanks out on the prairie, but here amongst people, my suspicion was that everyone was noticing, even though I knew that wasn't so. I set the sack on the floor, slid it into the corner with the toe of my boot, and took a seat.

Faster than a Baldwin locomotive down a long straightaway, a youngish man in a greasy apron came from the back room. He wore an eager, hungry look on his face that made me wonder if business was always this slow. "What will it be, mister?" He had blue eyes, sandy hair, and a ruddy complexion about his chin and jaw as if shaving didn't agree with him. I made him out to be in his mid-twenties.

I studied a hand-written menu propped between the salt and pepper shakers and quickly calculated my financial situation, which had been worsened considerably by recent expenses.

The liver and onions was eighteen cents and coffee, three cents. That fell right in line with my budget, and so I placed the order.

"I'll get your coffee right out to you, mister." He dashed back to the kitchen, where I glimpsed a woman stirring a big black pot of soup or stew, or something. She was young, too, and it was plain the two of them worked hard trying to make a go of the place.

While I waited for the coffee, I pulled out my pouch and counted up my remaining operating capital, satisfied there was enough to see me through to Fort Leavenworth, where I expected my meager fortune would turn a big corner. While out hunting, money had never been an issue. The few towns I'd passed through along the way had only cut marginally into my thin resources because I'd been prudent. I grinned, thinking about that. If my resources had been fatter, I wouldn't have needed to go hunting in the first place.

The man delivered the coffee, and not long after he set down a plate of liver and fried onions. The strong odor was pleasant indeed. As the cook refilled my coffee cup, I said, "Nice little town you got here." I really wasn't very impressed with Bend City, but it seemed the proper thing for a visitor like me to say.

"Think so?" His harsh tone came unexpected. He followed it with a short laugh and said, "I'm this close to pulling up roots and leaving." He illustrated with a thumb and forefinger.

"Are you indeed? I've only been in town an hour or so, and already I've got the impression that leaving seems to be the general goal of most folks in Bend City. What's stopping you?"

He laughed again, and this time the sound wore a bitter edge. "What stops anyone from doing anything? Money. Me and Margaret sank every penny we had into this café. This Dakota Territory is a nasty place come winter. Even worse come the spring rains. The mosquitoes will eat you alive, and if they don't get you, that river will—someday."

"Why'd you come here in the first place?" I asked.

He glanced at the plate-glass window that gave a glimpse of

the river below. "It wasn't too bad in the beginning. There was some money to be made early on, supplying wood to the steamers passing by. Lots of men and lots of business early on, but now the area is mostly timbered out."

"So I noticed. Reckon trees can be cut down faster than you can grow 'em."

"That's a fact, mister. White folks are moving out, and the Cheyenne, the peaceable ones that is, are moving in." He grimaced. "And Indians have no money to buy a meal from me."

"Is there anybody in this town not looking for a way out?"

The man thought a moment. "Bob Parker across the street seems to be holding on okay, although he grumbles a lot and sometimes talks of leaving, too. His saloon is not as busy as it was a year ago. The Indians somehow manage to find money for whiskey, which Parker sells to them in spite of that he's not supposed to.

"Henry Hagmann does all right. He owns a fish-salting business down by the river. He's a smart one, that man. He's taught the Cheyenne to fish for him. He gives them a couple flatboats and the gear and pays them a dime a day for all they can catch. The Indians turn around and spend that dime at Parker's saloon."

"Sounds like a pretty handsome deal for both men," I said. "What about the hardware store? It seems pretty well stocked for a town about to go bust."

"Walter Mace came to town about eight months ago, about the same time Mr. Hagmann arrived. He's what you might call an optimist. He says we're fixing to have us a building boom, and he's filling up his store like that prophecy is a foregone certainty. Personally, I suspect he's going to find himself all alone in a ghost town sitting on his mountain of nails, waiting for a boom that will never come. One day that old river will rile up and wash him and his nails down to the City of Kansas."

He might have read my mind. I laughed. "I suspect you're correct on that matter, sir."

CHAPTER 3

Shadows were pushing toward the river when I stepped out of the Big Muddy and stood on the sidewalk. Fall lurked just around the corner, and the air had cooled some. Except for that certain lingering odor from the sack in my hand, the air smelled clean. There wouldn't be much to do for the next day or two, I decided ruefully. That thought should have been welcomed. It wasn't. I wanted to be on my way. I had business to transact in Fort Leavenworth, and, afterward, I could go home. I'd been away a long time, and there were folks back there I missed—well, one in particular.

I grimaced and tried not to think about Francine. Recalling her pretty face would only make the time pass slower. I started across the street, dodging road apples. Apparently Bend City either did not have the funds or did not see the need to hire a street sweeper.

Who'd've ever thought a man would yearn for a street sweeper?

The call of civilization was rising up inside me. I gave a wry grin and hoped one of those unscheduled steamers would make an appearance soon. Climbing the steps to the boardwalk on the other side of the street put me in front of the Buffalo Wallow Saloon. Past the batwing doors I saw that the place was practically empty but for three white men and an equal number of Injuns. With the ten cents a day Henry Hagmann was paying his Injuns, I could see how Parker's place wouldn't be making much of a go of it. I made a mental recount of my remaining money. There was enough for my and Blue Shanks's room and board, a couple more meals for me, steerage passage for us as far as Fort Leavenworth, and a bit left over for a couple of drinks . . . later.

I felt the need to stretch my legs, and since folks passing by had begun staring and widening the distance between me and them, I turned toward River Street . . . and came up short, face to face with that same Injun in the grubby, red shirt. I stepped to one side. He stepped, too. I moved left, and, like we was dancing, he moved, too.

"What?" I asked

"Whiskey." He held out a hand, his eyes oddly fixed upon my face.

"Can't you take a hint, Chief?" I dodged to my right and managed to scoot past him, taking the road down to the river in long strides. When I looked over my shoulder, he was standing there watching me.

The wharf was mostly deserted, the sawmill down at the far end silent now. A small flock of herons strode about the muddy shallows poking their long beaks into the water and then gulping down little fish.

Near the southernmost pier three small flatboats had tied up. From them a dozen or so Cheyenne were busily filling a wheelbarrow with fish.

I slapped my neck. My hand showed a bloody smear and the smudge of a smashed mosquito. All at once a black cloud of the little buggers descended upon me. I swatted my way out of the cloud and walked out onto the north pier, past the couple small boats moored alongside it that I'd noticed earlier. I stood at its end looking up and down the river. Slanting sunlight glanced off the slow, brown water. The mighty Missouri was sleeping this afternoon, but that was only a ruse to put the people who lived along her banks off their guard. One day this beast would wake up. It'd stir and stretch itself, and on that day all of Bend City would become a memory.

Quite unexpectedly I thought of Francine. My heart got heavy even as a smile came to my face. What was it the cook had said? *What stops anyone from doing anything? Money.*

My fingers tightened around the sack in my fist. When this was all over, money wouldn't be a problem.

I sighed and looked up river, hoping to spy a plume of smoke rising in the evening air. But the darkening sky was clear, and the only sounds were not that of a steam whistle, but of chattering Injun fishermen off-loading their flatboats.

Approaching the corner of River and Main, I slowed and sidled up alongside the saloon, peeking around front. Chief was sitting on a bench near the door. I had suspected as much. He appeared to be napping . . . or maybe he was setting a trap for me?

I took a chance, strode quickly past him, and dove into the saloon, the batwing doors slapping closed behind me.

The place was dark, and I moved to one side waiting for my eyes to adjust. A balding man with a big belly straining his white apron stood on a step stool lighting the lamps in an iron chandelier. Along one wall a pair of heavy timbers stretching across three barrels served as a bar. A shelf behind it held a few bottles and glasses. A dusty mirror hung at an angle. At the end of the bar the door to a back room stood ajar, a weak light coming from it. I counted eight tables, two of them occupied—one with white men and the other with Injuns. Six stools stood before the bar, three of them in use.

Peanut shells cracked under my boots as I crossed the room and took a stool at the end of the bar.

Once every lamp in the place was ablaze, the barman came over. He had a pleasant smile. In the low light, I saw that the man's eyes were bright blue, and quick as a thimblerigger's shuffle.

"Whiskey?" He grinned half apologetically. "The answer better be yes 'cause I'm all outta beer until the next riverboat brings me new stock."

"In that case, I think I'll have a whiskey." I wasn't much of a whiskey drinker, but I doubted a saloon in a backwater place like Bend City would stock a good brand of Madeira, or even a decent bottle of brandy.

The bartender said, "Waiting for a timely shipment on this river is like waiting for water to boil." He laughed and splashed a couple of fingers of liquid from an unmarked bottle into a glass, spilling some on the bar. "I ain't seen your face around," he said wiping the spill with a corner of his apron. "Just get in?"

"A couple hours ago." It felt a lot longer than that.

"Planning to stay?"

"No longer than it takes for the next steamer down river to show up."

"Smart man." The barman's eyelids lowered, and his nostrils began working the air like a hound on a scent. "Some critter must have crawled under the building again and died."

I feigned innocence—"Hate it when that happens"—and tasted the whiskey. A bit of watering down had obviously taken place, likely in order to stretch a dwindling stock until the next shipment arrived.

A monster mosquito landed on the barman's beefy forearm, and immediately the pesky insect went about its business. A swift slap ended the mosquito's enterprise, distracting the barman from further investigating the smell.

He fished around under the bar, coming up with an armful of flower vases filled with dried cattails and commenced to using a few matches to light them afire. When he got them punks smoking like a chimney he set them about the saloon, and soon those smoldering cattails filled the place with a hazy, mosquito-repelling smoke. They also served to mask the odor of the "critter that had died under the building."

I sipped my drink and thought about home . . . and Francine. Those thoughts naturally gave way to money and what I was going to do once I actually had any. First I'd buy a new suit, and then, dressed like gentry—like her pa—I'd ask for Francine's hand. With the fat bank account that was practically mine already, how could he refuse me?

My thoughts wandered. When I glanced out the window again, night had arrived. A few lights showed in the windows across the street, and the saloon had taken in a few more customers. Some faces I recognized. Toby McGill, the stableman, drifted in and took a seat at a table with the restaurateur I'd met earlier. A third fellow I hadn't seen before joined them.

The freight clerk, Irwin Wert, came in for a moment, spoke to a couple of fellows at the far end of the bar, and then the three of them left.

I ordered another watered-down whiskey and carefully counted the money in my pouch. I could book steerage passage for probably a few dollars. Boats going south often had plenty of room, their cargo having been off-loaded upriver. I added it all up in my head again, threw in ten percent for good measure, and calculated I had seven dollars more than I'd need to make it to Fort Leavenworth.

My view slanted toward the table where McGill and the others sat playing what appeared to be a friendly game of poker. It wasn't the game so much that interested me. I'd been alone on Bill Riley's trail so long, the thought of a few hours of human companionship was almost irresistible.

I carried the sack, my saddlebags, carbine, and drink over to the table and stood near a fourth chair.

"Evening, gentlemen. Mr. McGill, nice to see you again. I

trust Miss Blue Shanks has comfortable arrangements."

"Why, hello . . . Mr. Ragland, is it not?"

"It is indeed." I was pleased he remembered my name.

"Your mare has taken to stable life like fleas to an Injun war bonnet," McGill declared.

The men chuckled, and McGill made introductions. The restaurateur, whom I'd met earlier, was Franklin Collins, and the third fellow was Henry Hagmann. I recognized the name.

"You run the fish works down by the wharf."

"You are an observant fellow, Mr. Ragland."

Collins nodded to the empty chair. "Pull up and have a seat, Mr. Ragland."

"A prudent man would first inquire into what sort of stakes you gentleman are playin' for? I'm a mite thin on cash at the moment."

Hagmann, shuffling the deck, said, "Straight poker, nickel ante, nickel first raise, sky's the limit after that." His gray eyes glinted, and he chuckled to show me that he was only joking—well, maybe half joking. I couldn't read Hagmann as clearly as I could McGill and Collins.

"Them's the kind of stakes I can live with," I said setting the sack, my saddlebags, and carbine on the floor under the chair.

"No boat yet, Mr. Ragland?" McGill asked, making small talk as he collected his cards. We each tossed a nickel into the pot.

"I've been advised that they arrive on an irregular schedule."

Hagmann huffed. "That's the truth. Impossible to run a profitable business when you never know when to expect your transportation."

Collins studied his cards. "Instead of complaining, do something about it."

"Do what? Close up shop and move down river like the others? No thanks. I make out okay even with the inconveniences."

Keeping his eyes on the cards, Collins said, "I'm a cat's whisker away from jumping ship."

"You've been saying that for months now," Hagmann grumbled.

McGill laughed. "Don't fret, Frankie, you're not the only fool who got suckered into sinking good money into Bend City."

I concentrated on my cards, only half listening to their banter. Bend City wasn't my problem. I had no stake here.

I won the first hand and pulled the money over to my side of the table. "What is it about this place that's got folks moving out?"

Collins gathered the cards up. "Like I told you earlier, regular folks keep moving out and the Cheyenne keep moving in. Except for the few who work for Henry here, none has any money except what they get through street begging."

"Met one of 'em this afternoon," I said.

McGill said, "I think Mr. Ragland wants to know why white folk begun moving out in the first place."

Collins began the deal. "That's because . . . aw shucks, that's just an old Indian legend. Just plain foolishness." He looked over his shoulder and then back and lowered his voice. "Ain't no truth to them legends. And if I had more than two pennies to rub together, I'd be out of here too, like Harel and Alice done yesterday." He looked at me. "They had a bake shop down on West Sawmill Road. Alice claimed Indians from the graveyard would come stalking through their bedroom in the middle of the night."

I collected my cards. "That's mighty brazen of 'em. Why didn't she just shoot 'em?"

McGill said, " 'Cause they's weren't live Indians. They's weren't even Cheyenne. They's the ghosts of what some around here call the *First Ones*. They's used to have a village right here where Bend City sets now. That was a long time ago, centuries before the Cheyenne moved in. There's a bunch of them buried up in the cemetery. No one knew they's were there until the first graves were dug. Now whenever we find an old bone, we bury it in the corner of the cemetery where there were some standing stones with old Indian carvings."

Injun ghosts. I just smiled and didn't say anything. It seems about every other frontier town in this whole western land is built atop an old Injun graveyard.

I lost the next hand, but I was still up twenty cents and feeling pretty good. The saloon keeper came around with a bottle, inquiring as to our liquor needs.

Henry Hagmann generously paid for drinks all around.

Our conversation rambled. I learned more about the town, its ancient ghosts, and the very generous Wally Mace, who had bought out Harel and Alice's business so as they could pull up roots and find somewhere else to earn a living.

Now and then someone would sniff the air and wrinkle his nose, but Bobby Parker kept the punks burning in his war against the mosquitoes, and that kept anyone from pointing a finger at the greasy burlap sack under my chair.

Sometime later Parker came inquiring again, bottle in hand. Lady Luck seemed to have taken a shine to me. Having played a string of winning hands, I bought the table a round. Watered down or not, the whiskey was loosening us up. Nickel antes became dime antes, and then two bits.

Fickle as ever, Lady Luck sashayed around the table to the next fellow. Hagmann took a couple of big pots, and then Collins managed to win a few dollars. McGill held even, taking in about as much as he gave out. He didn't seem to care. It was plain that McGill, like me, was in the game for the camaraderie. The stableman and I shared the same problem. We both spent too much time around livestock.

I calculated my wins and losses. I was up for the night, and if

I stayed in the game long enough, I was pretty sure Miss Luck would come back around and whisper in my ear again.

Sure enough. A couple of hands later she was leaning over my shoulder and smiling down on me, blowing magic kisses as the cards came my way. They were all red . . . all diamonds . . . all . . . my breath caught and my heart kicked me hard in the ribs as I gathered them into my hand . . . ace to a ten.

I counted and recounted and then counted them all again, trying hard not to sweat or give away any telltales. Hagmann was watching me. I still hadn't figured out how to read the man. So was Collins. McGill had his eyes bent toward the cards in his hand, but the corners of his lips had begun to creep up.

McGill led off, pushing two bits across the table. We'd long ago abandoned the nickel ante.

Collins matched and raised a dollar. He was holding a strong hand, but not as strong as mine. I stared at the royal flush, hardly believing my good fortune, trying not to show it on my face as I met Collins's raise and raised it another dollar.

Hagmann's suspicious view shot toward me, narrowed, and then dipped toward his cards, eyebrows crawling together into a fuzzy V as he chewed the corner of his lip. After some deliberation, he saw the bet but didn't raise. It was a cautious move. I sensed that the fish merchant's reluctance was only a ruse to see if I'd been bluffing.

McGill looked worried and called for another card. It must have been the one he wanted. Fighting to keep a blank face, he dug into a pocket and tossed a bright twenty-dollar coin into the pot.

Collins sucked air through his teeth and folded. "Too rich for me."

It was my turn. Although I was sitting in the catbird seat, a twinge of panic pinched my chest. Even holding an unbeatable hand, I could lose the play if the pot grew bigger than I could cover.

"Well?" Hagmann prodded.

I quickly re-evaluated my finances. The pile of coins stacked at my elbow lacked nine dollars of McGill's bold, twenty-dollar raise.

"Folding?" Hagmann asked with an irritating hint of glee.

"No," I barked and pulled the money pouch from my pocket. Eleven dollars and twenty cents—riverboat passage, food, and my and Blue Shanks's rooming expenses—all the money I had left. I put it all on the table. "See your raise and raise you two dollars and twenty cents."

I was full tapped out. Every penny of my current net worth lay there before my eyes. I took a long breath to settle my nerves and reminded myself that nothing beats a royal flush.

Now it was Hagmann's turn to look worried. He brooded over his cards and after much deliberation produced two gold coins. "Getting kind of interesting." The coins clinked atop the pile. "That's to cover McGill's raise, your raise, and seventeen dollars and eighty cents more." He smiled. "I'm calling your bluff, Mr. Ragland."

I swept off my hat and shoved my fingers through my hair. The saloon went out of focus and the room did sort of a jig as I stared at the pot. Maybe it was Parker's watered-down whiskey getting to me? I didn't want to believe what my eyes were telling me. My fears had come true! The pot had grown taller than I could reach.

CHAPTER 4

His thin smile slowly widening, Hagmann watched me like a worm he'd cleverly skewered on his hook. He shifted his view toward McGill, who was doing some serious squirming himself.

McGill's eyes flicked from the pile of coins on the table to the cards in his hand and then back again, pinpricks of perspiration popping out across his forehead. He slowly dipped a hand into his pocket, came out with another double eagle, but then hesitated, his turmoil plain. "Ah, fiddles!" He shoved the coin back into his pocket and slapped the cards face down on the table. "Martha will hang me on a meat hook if she ever hears how much money I lost tonight."

"Ha-ha-ha." Hagmann speared me with a victorious stare. "And I suspect you're tapped out, too, Mr. Ragland."

His gloating rankled almost as badly as the idea of losing every penny I had while holding a winning hand! "Let me think a minute," I snapped. There had to be a way out for me.

"Go ahead. Take two minutes, if you think it'll help any."

I turned to Collins. "Cover this bet for me, and I'll split the pot with you."

Collins threw up his hands like as much to fend off a wild Comanche. "No, sir. Money's too hard to come by these days, and I've the same problem as Toby. My woman pinches pennies, too. No, I'm out of this hand."

I glanced at McGill. "Same offer."

The stableman shook his head and shoved his chair back as if

34

the act of widening the distance between him and me would somehow protect him from the temptation. "Sorry, I'm burned already. Time for me to step back from the fire."

Hagmann pushed out his chest. "Well, looks like *my* missus will be right pleased when *I* come through the door." He reached for the pot.

I said, "Wait."

"For what?" Hagmann asked. "You're out of money."

Desperate situations required bold moves, although I might regret it come morning. I had no choice. I reached under my chair. The burlap sack gave a loud thump when I plopped it onto the table, right on top of the pile of coins there.

What followed was something akin to a human tidal wave as a swell of curious spectators rolled in for a closer look. Almost immediately they rolled out again, the saloon filling with groans of disgust as the freshly disturbed hemp fibers released their pent-up volume of stink into the close quarters.

No amount of smoky punks could mask that odor. It was the smell of death, and every man there knew it.

Henry Hagmann scraped back his chair and shot to his feet, staring at the grimy sack as if any moment he expected it to up and bite him. "What's in there?"

Every eye in the saloon had turned toward me, and I felt like the bearded lady in a traveling carnival. A wariness had silenced them. They seemed to be waiting for something dramatic and possible deadly to befall them.

I had their attention, as unwelcome as it was, so I played the moment to its fullest, most dramatic effect, saying boldly, "I see your raise, Mr. Hagmann."

"What?" Hagmann grew more disturbed with each tick of the clock, which could be clearly heard due to the deathly silence that had come over the place. "Are you serious, man? What is it you have there? A dead coon?"

"Only my dinner. Well, in a manner of speaking, it's many dinners." I grinned and untied the mouth of the sack. Hesitating, I grimaced and reached inside, drawing out a bundle wrapped in canvas and bailing twine. I turned my head aside from the stench as I sliced the twine with my big Bowie knife and peeled back the wrapper.

The saloon gave a collective gasp at the sight of the human head there in the middle of the table, staring up at the ceiling from sunken eye sockets. Shrunken skin emphasized the man's cheekbones and drew the corners of his frozen lips up in a grotesque grin. A wiggling clump of white maggots had already begun to occupy the long, dried gash that my first bullet had cut along the skull, just below his coarse, red hairline.

Someone got sick and rushed out into the street. The wrenching sound of his vomiting seemed an appropriate exclamation mark at the end of a gruesome sentence. Slowly the more inquisitive of them began to breathe again and moved in for a closer look, and with that came the questions.

Hagmann shot me a narrow stare. "Who is this man?"

"His name is—was—Bill Riley."

The saloon was instantly abuzz. Not a man there didn't recognize the name of the infamous gunman who for the last five years had terrorized folks from Omaha clear up to Bismarck.

Disgust turned to curiosity, and men pressed in closer for another look, in spite of the smell.

"That sorta looks like him," someone ventured.

The saloon keeper pushed his way through the crowd with a roll of papers. Thumbing through them he pulled one out of the bunch and spread a dog-eared wanted poster on the table next to the head. "That sure enough is Bill Riley. It says right here he's worth two thousand five hundred dollars, dead or alive."

"That's an old poster, Mr. Parker." I opened my saddlebag and pulled out one I'd picked up at the City of Kansas landing.

36

The picture was more recent and better drawn. I said, "The price on Bill Riley's head is up to three thousand dollars. Payable in gold at Fort Leavenworth, Kansas." I gave Hagmann a grin. "I'm not asking for you to meet that amount, Mr. Hagmann; only that you allow Mr. Riley here to cover your raise. Is that agreeable with you?"

Hagmann stammered. "Let me think a minute."

The tables had turned. I was in control of the situation again, and that's how I liked it. "Go ahead. Take two minutes, if you think it'll help any."

". . . after that I picked up their trail along the Grand River and dogged them south for nearly a week. The ground was gumbo mud, and they left tracks even an Easterner could follow."

"That wasn't too smart of 'em," said one of the dozen or so men who'd gathered around me to hear the story of how I killed Bill Riley.

I nodded. "Bill Riley was meaner than raw corn liquor, but he was a pretty dim lamp. His two yahoo saddle partners weren't what you'd call bright candles either, but they was pure evil.

"The trail led to a soddy. By the time I got there, the man and his wife inside were dead. Bill Riley had murdered them both and cleaned out what canned goods he could find."

Someone said, "Old Bill Riley was the devil himself."

The crowd that pressed around the table mumbled their agreement.

I wasn't normally so full of words, but once the shock of seeing Bill Riley's sunken eyes had passed, curiosity overcame the stench, and they had insisted on hearing how it had come about that I, T. J. Ragland, had killed the most famous outlaw in the territory. Parker's watered-down whiskey had loosened my tongue a mite, too, and now more of the same was coming my way from admirers who looked upon me with new-found awe that hadn't been there fifteen minutes earlier.

I continued. "A cold rain blew through, and I holed up for a day under my oilcloth till it passed. The rain fairly washed away their tracks, but I was too dang close to catching up with them to lose them again. I began cutting back and forth and soon picked up their trail where they'd crossed the north fork of the Cheyenne River.

"It led me into the mountains the Sioux call the Paha Sapa. That's when I caught a whiff of smoke. Worried it might be the Sioux, as I'd been warned they live thereabouts, I crept down into a deep gulch so snarled with dead wood it nearly put an end to my enterprise. I was about to backtrack and search for another way down when I spied a curl of smoke about a hundred yards below, where Riley and his partners had made camp along a creek.

"Crawling through the tangle of downed timber, I come to a place that gave me a clear view of them. They were acting mighty peculiar, all three of them. Had their trouser legs rolled up and were splashing about the creek with their boots still on, peering down like they were hunting minnows. Ever now and again one of them would dip down and fish up a tiny stone and declare, 'Found another one,' or, 'Got a big one.' They seemed mighty excited about those little rocks."

"What was they finding in that creek?" Franklin Collins asked.

I shrugged. "Never got a chance to ask them."

Collins's eyes took on a faraway gaze.

"You see, they were so busy playing in the water that they never heard me come into camp. I crouched behind their tent, watching a while. One of 'em was Big Nose Cassidy, but the other one was unfamiliar to me. Far as I knew, Cassidy had no money on his head.

"After watching a while, I stepped out in plain sight and stood on the bank. Even then, it took a full minute before anyone spied me standing there, my saddle carbine resting in the crook of my arm."

The men around the table were listening with wide-eyed interest. Even Henry Hagmann looked mesmerized. Their attention was flattering, but it made me skittish, too. I was a quiet man by nature, and being the center of interest—the bearded lady in a traveling carnival—was not the sort of notoriety I craved.

"What happened next?" a toothless fellow with gray, wiry whiskers asked.

"Well, when they finally spotted me, Bill Riley and his partners went stone still, too surprised to say anything at first. I said, 'Look at you three there dripping like wet laundry on a line, and it ain't even Saturday.' Of course, I had no idea what day of the week it was, and I suspect they didn't neither.

"Riley was the first to speak. 'Who the hell are you?'

" 'Ragland's the name. T. J. And I come to take you to Fort Leavenworth. Some folks there want to meet you and are willing to pay for the opportunity.'

"Bill Riley's view slid slyly toward a bleached tree trunk near the creek bank where a couple of rifles leaned. I acted like I didn't notice. His eyes came right back to me. 'You a bounty hunter?'

" 'It's honest work at least. You and your partners here have not made the job easy.'

"Riley laughed, and his two partners began to slowly drift apart. 'You don't expect two thousand dollars to just fall into your pocket, do you?'

"Big Nose Cassidy, moving like a snail across a cold rock, inched closer to the guns. I pretended not to notice.

"I laughed. 'You've been away too long. I bring good news, Mr. Riley. The price has gone up a mite.'

"Riley shoved a hand into his pocket and looked pleased.

'How much?' He turned his back on Big Nose to keep my eyes from going there.

" 'Three thousand. Dead or alive.'

"He thought that over. 'Dead will make it a lot easier.'

" 'So I suspect.'

"The other fellow hadn't moved. 'I'm not worth nothing, alive or dead,' he declared.

"I glanced at him, keeping Big Nose in the corner of my eye. 'Reckon that's so. I've no interest in you.' They were trying to distract me with their talk. Big Nose was almost to the creek bank. My chest and shoulders began to tighten, waiting on his next move.

"Quick as a snake, Riley's hand came out of his pocket and flung a handful of those little rocks they'd been gathering at me. The unnamed fellow dodged to my right. That was the signal I'd been waiting for. I spun left. Big Nose had grabbed a rifle and was swinging toward me. My carbine was still in my elbow. I squeezed off a shot, hit him low, and spun him. He came around, tossing Riley a revolver with one hand and firing his rifle with the other. His bullet went wide. Mine took his throat out.

"Riley had caught the revolver by the barrel midair and was fumbling it right way 'round. I worked the lever, skinned him with my first shot and killed him with a second.

"The third fellow, he threw up his hands, trembling like a bride on her wedding night."

A low chuckle drifted across the saloon. More folks had been coming in off the street to see what the attraction was. Bobby Parker was hopping, busy filling glasses and pocketing money.

"I told the fellow to shuck his boots and git. He seemed mighty happy to do so, skedaddling just as fast as his stockinged feet would carry him over the gravel bar and into the timber.

"Found their hobbled horses and set them loose. I didn't see the need to haul all of Bill Riley back to Leavenworth, seeing the head alone would suffice." I drew my big officer's Bowie from its steel sheath and showed it to them. "I unburdened his head from his body with this."

The whiskered codger gave a whistle. "That's a pretty blade." I let him look it over, and he passed it around to some of the other men there.

It came back to me, and I slipped it back into the dented sheath that had rode on my belt since the War. "So there you have the story of how I killed Bill Riley." I slanted my view across the table at Henry Hagmann. "Well, what have you decided, Mr. Hagmann?"

Hagmann nodded. "I will allow for Bill Riley's head to cover the bet. Why don't you show us your hand, Mr. Ragland."

CHAPTER 5

"Royal flush!" The oldster with the wiry beard declared when I laid out my cards.

Hagmann stared at them, a slow grin moving across his face. "That's a rare hand indeed. I can see why you would risk Mr. Riley here." He laughed and ordered another round of drinks for the table.

"Figured one of these days my luck would turn." I pulled the pile of coins over to my side.

Bobby Parker stood nearby gripping the whiskey bottle, eagerly filling glasses and pocketing the coins being pushed at him. His eyes darted between the withering head and the crowd of men streaming in off the street to see Bill Riley. Word had apparently gotten around.

Parker approached me a little nervously. "Er, Mr. Ragland? You wouldn't consider selling old Bill there, would you?"

His offer came as a surprise. I paused, my hands still wrapped about the pile of coins. "Well, I would indeed, Mr. Parker. For about three thousand dollars."

Parker grimaced. "I was hoping we might come to an agreement for somewhat less than that, Mr. Ragland." By the apologetic tone in his voice, I knew he was thinking quite a bit less. "I've got six hundred dollars put away to pay for my next shipment of libations, but I'll hand it over to you tonight, right now, for Mr. Riley there." He added quickly, "You'd have cash in hand and wouldn't have to bother hauling that gruesome thing all the way back to Fort Leavenworth."

I considered his offer for all of maybe five seconds. The idea of parting ways with Bill Riley had a genuine appeal, but I shook my head anyway. "Thanks for the offer, but six hundred is considerably below the going rate for a Bill Riley head. I'll just see this grisly task through to the end, thank you."

"Oh, I understand. It's just that"—Parker's view skimmed the faces crowding the saloon, nearly bursting at the seams— "just that Mr. Riley would be good for business, if you get my drift."

I did. Parker figured he'd discovered a way to double or triple business by putting the head on display and then advertising. It made business sense. Some men are born to be businessmen, and others are destined to be paupers. Parker was definitely one of the former. I said, "I see how that might be, but Mr. Riley is coming with me."

Parker shrugged. "It was worth a try."

For a long time after that men drifted into the saloon for a look at Bill Riley. As a good-will gesture, I let Bobby Parker prop Bill on a ledge behind his bar where everyone had a clear view of him. Parker had fished up a crayon from behind the bar, scribbled an advertisement on the back of one of the wanted posters, and hung it in the window. That pulled in a few more men eager for a glimpse of Bill Riley.

I took a stool at the bar where I could keep an eye on my investment, and for the rest of the night my drinks were on the house. I took advantage of Bobby Parker's generosity—maybe more than I should have.

In spite of my normally retiring nature, I made a lot of new acquaintances and spied some older ones. Franklin Collins wanted to hear again about the place where I'd caught up with Bill Riley. And Irwin Wert had come back to the saloon, congratulated me on my good luck, and then went off and sat with a few other gents, casting a glance my way every now and again.

It was late when I finally wrapped the smelly head back in its oilcloth wrapper, shoved it into the burlap sack, and staggered off the stool, glad-handing my way toward the batwings. Friendly back-pats ushered me out the door into the night.

On the dark boardwalk, swaying a bit, I filled my lungs with the fresh air off the river. I felt large and strong—a man of worth! I grinned at that thought, took a step, and fell against the wall. I'd had too much to drink and not enough to eat. As a precaution, I tied the sack around by wrist so's I wouldn't drop it.

My belly gurgled as I steadied myself and pointed my feet homeward. I hadn't gone five steps when a now-familiar voice asked, "Whiskey?"

I strained to focus on the dirty, red shirt. My blurred gaze climbed past the cheap glass beads to the swarthy face framed in long, greasy, black hair. "Don't you ever sleep, Chief?"

"Me want whiskey."

I laughed and hooked a thumb over my shoulder. "Probably not that watered-down stuff served in there."

Chief didn't smile. Maybe he hadn't understood all that? I shrugged. The evening had been good to me, and I had a pouch fat with coins. "If I give you a nickel, will you go away and leave me alone?"

Chief only stared.

"Well, I've had me a dandy evening at the table. Reckon I can share the wealth a mite." I fished around inside a pocket and came out with a coin. A full quarter-dollar, but I was too drunk to care and slapped it into Chief's open palm. "There you go."

Without even a thank-you, the Injun aimed his moccasins at the batwing doors and disappeared inside. I grinned and, clutching my sack tighter, started home. The air had taken on a fall chill, bringing wisps of fog up from the river below.

I staggered along the sidewalk toward the end of town where my rented room and feather pillow called to me, the poker game and camaraderie a blurred but comfortable memory. Coming to Sawmill Road I braced myself against a porch upright to get my bearings and steady my legs for the three long steps down to the road and then pushed off to begin my descent.

Right about then something came down hard on my head. I didn't feel any pain, only a mind-numbing jolt. The rough wood of the boardwalk rushed up to meet my face.

And then nothing.

Consciousness returned in fits and starts.

It was dark all around me.

My head felt stuck between the jaws of a vise with little green gnomes hopping up and down on the screw lever. Slowly I became aware of a deep ache in my left shoulder. My back and legs seemed to be afire. I tried to move, but something pinned me to the ground. I went cautiously still, breathing deeply in spite of a gagging stench in my nose, my heartbeat drumming in my ears.

Other than my heartbeat, which I was thankful to be hearing, the world around me remained silent. I tried again to move.

The stench, I discovered, was vomit.

My vision cleared a little. I was wedged tight, my one shoulder crushed against the rough stones of a foundation, the other against a hogshead. My left leg seemed to be twisted under my back with something like a hot poker stabbing my knee. Carefully, I straightened my leg, grimacing as the burn raced down to my tingling toes.

With a groan, I extracted myself and sat against the hogshead trying to collect my thoughts, shivering in the chilling river fog that swirled around me. Plainly someone had knocked me out and dumped me here out of sight. Why? My thoughts were muddled . . . and then an explosion of clarity brought everything into sharp focus.

The sack!

I felt for it. When it didn't immediately fall to hand, panic took hold, and I made a desperate search. I found my carbine and saddlebags, but Bill Riley was gone.

I made my way down to the riverbank and washed off the vomit the best I could. My stomach had stopped gurgling at least, but my head throbbed horribly.

In the dark I sat on a log by the sawmill, trying to sort through my thoughts, trying to make a plan. From time to time I drank from the river to slake the horrible dryness in my mouth. Across the river the sky began to brighten. Sometime later workers began arriving at the sawmill. I collected my stuff and moved stiffly away from there, my legs heavy as if mired in molasses. I'd lost Bill Riley. Three thousand dollars gone. I'd been drunk. Drunk and confident. If I hadn't been, I'd have been more aware of my surroundings. And I'd still have Bill Riley.

Drunk and stupid!

The smell of Hagmann's Fishworks got my stomach to churning again. Fearing I'd puke, I left the wharf and trudged up River Street to Bend Avenue, where I paused, leaning against a post, staring at the Buffalo Wallow Saloon's closed door. A great wave of regret washed over me again. I turned away and made my way toward the marshal's office.

Few people were out and about this early, and none I recognized from the night before. I doubted the marshal could do any better than me in finding my stolen property, but figured I ought to declare the theft anyway.

The door was open, catching the morning sunlight. The

shingle above it read: *B. Bulger, Deputy Territorial Marshal.*

The place was sparsely furnished: a desk neatly arranged, a couple of chairs, a territorial map on the wall, a rifle rack with a Winchester and a shotgun. Two flat-strap iron jail cells stood in a back corner, neither one occupied. The only person there was a cleaning woman, busily sweeping the floor.

She looked up when I came in, and the broom stopped. Her nose wrinkled, a sudden scowl scrunching her face. It wasn't a bad looking face. She was maybe forty, judging by the gray streaks in her hair. She wasn't a large woman. A strong wind might carry her away. I couldn't tell for sure, but her eyes looked to be some shade of green.

"What happened to you?" she said sharply.

I looked down at myself, embarrassed by the stain on my shirt that the river water couldn't quite wash away. "Guess I had me a little case of spew."

"You're drunk."

I winced. "Not so much anymore."

"Don't expect any sympathy from me."

"No, ma'am. I don't. And I apologize for my present condition. It's not a manner in which I prefer to present myself, especially to a lady such as you."

Her demeanor softened the tiniest little bit. "What is it I can do for you?" she asked.

I glanced about the office. "Well, ma'am, I'm looking for Marshal Bulger."

Her back stiffened ever so slightly, and her view narrowed. "I am Marshal Bulger."

That threw me off guard. Law enforcement was certainly different here in the territories. I quickly removed my hat. "Sorry, ma'am. Never met a lady peace officer before. Never heard of such a thing."

Her face hardened. "Now you have. And put that hat back on

your head. No need to treat me any different from a man. I'm doing a man's job. What is it you want?"

I detected a bitter note. "I want to report a robbery . . . assault and robbery, to be exact."

"Who was robbed?"

"Me."

"And the assault?"

"Whoever done it knocked me out." My hand moved to the back of my head and tenderly touched the knob of flesh there. "And then they stuffed me in the alley by the Methodist Church where nobody would see."

"I suppose that *might* explain your filthy clothes."

"And my spew," I added.

"No, that was whiskey. Your breath reeks of it." Her eyes narrowed, and her voice took on a reprimanding note. " 'Wine is a mocker, strong drink is raging. Whosoever is deceived thereby is not wise.' Bear that in mind."

I winced. The Good Book also spoke of judging and judging not, but I wasn't about to argue scripture with her, as I knew she was right.

Her tone mellowed some. "What was stolen?"

"It was. It was . . ." How to describe it? I figured I just had to flat out say it. "It was a head. Human."

Marshal Bulger's eyes got big, and she stabbed a finger at me. "You. You're Ragland. You're the one who killed Bill Riley."

I nodded, amazed at how quickly my fame had spread. "There's a three-thousand-dollar bounty on Riley."

"Yes, I know. I heard the talk as I was making my rounds last night. Got the whole story how you tracked Riley out on the gumbo plains and bushwhacked him and his partners, Big Nose Cassidy and Jimmy Jake Rawlins."

That wasn't how it happened, but when I tried to give her the straight of it, she rushed on, "And then you went and cut the heads off all three of 'em and hauled 'em down to the Cheyenne and tossed the bodies into the river."

"That's not exactly . . ." Instinctively my hand went to the big knife on my belt, and I discovered it was missing, too.

"You're a mighty mean fellow, Ragland. At the very least you could have given those three yahoos a sporting chance."

"They went for their guns first," I said, still attempting to correct her misunderstanding of how it happened.

"Instead of back-shooting them like you done." She drew in a long breath, not having heard a word I'd said. "Don't know as there was any paper on Rawlins and Cassidy, but if they were riding with Riley, there ought to have been." She studied me a moment. "You done to them and now someone done to you. I say you made off better than those three."

I saw how she had the story fixed in her brain, and how she wouldn't hear the truth of it. "What are you going to do about it, Marshal?"

Bulger set the broom aside, slid onto the chair, and ruffled some papers on the desk. "I'll make a record of your report and do some investigating." She looked up at me. "I don't hold out much chance we'll be finding Bill Riley's head. Where're you staying?"

"I got a room above the hardware store."

"Wally Mace. Naturally. Where else would a stranger be staying?" she said as if talking to herself, writing it on a piece of paper. She looked up. "If I find the culprit, I'll arrest him."

"If I find him, he won't need arresting."

She shot me a warning look, and I noticed that her eyes were indeed green—a sort of putrid green, the color of scum that grows on stagnant water in the hot days of August. "This town is under my jurisdiction, Mr. Ragland. I'll take care of it." She looked back at the paper and continued writing. "Did they steal anything else?"

"My knife," I said, touching the empty scabbard and feeling oddly sad about that. I had no emotional tie to Bill Riley, but that knife had been at my side a long time.

Bulger went back to scribbling. "I'll let you know if I find out anything," she said, not looking up.

It was her way of dismissing me, and I felt like a schoolboy who'd just had a ruler slapped across his knuckles. I left there with little hope in sight. I had scant faith in a female lawman. B. Bulger, I was convinced, wasn't going to find Bill Riley's head.

CHAPTER 6

I left grumbling to myself. Going to the law had been a waste of time. I'd have to find Bill myself. And find him I would! Even if that meant searching every corner of this two-bit town.

My anger boiled as I stormed away from B. Bulger's office.

I stopped abruptly when a figure stepped in front of me and stuck out a hand.

"Whiskey."

"You again! Go away!" I pushed past the Injun, my boots thundering upon the boardwalk. I'd lost Bill Riley's head and my knife, my clothes were filthy, I smelled to high heaven of vomit . . . and I was hungry. In my anger, I strode right past the barber shop. It wasn't until I'd gone a couple steps that the words on a cardboard window sign pushed through the anger and registered in my brain. I dug in my heels and turned back.

Shave and Bath 40¢.

I looked at the window a little closer. On a pane of glass was painted: *Boyd Nattingwood. Barber, Dentist, Physician.* It seemed Mr. Nattingwood was a man of many talents.

I peeked through the window at the barber chair, unoccupied except for the barber himself reading a newspaper. My hand felt inside my pocket not expecting to find anything. To my surprise the full amount of my winnings was still there.

A scowl wrinkled my forehead. Either the thief had been careless or didn't know about the money . . . or he couldn't be bothered with what amounted to small change compared to what Bill Riley would bring.

At the jingle of the bell above the door, barber/doctor/dentist Nattingwood looked over the top of his newspaper. Recognition sparked a flame in his wide, brown eyes, and he bolted from the chair. "Well, well, Mr. Ragland!" He pumped my hand enthusiastically. Nattingwood had a deep, rich voice that reminded me of the stage actor who played Othello in a play I'd once seen in the Clark Street Theater. Maybe he could add *thespian* to his list of accomplishments?

I thought his face familiar—one of the dozen or so who'd crowded around the table last night, no doubt.

"I can sure use a bath and a shave, and maybe scrub my clothes."

"Of course!"

I dipped a hand into my pocket.

"And, of course, your money is no good here."

"I can pay." I'd never been comfortable taking charity.

"I know you can. You won the pot last night." The barber flashed a bright smile. "But I insist. It would be my honor to scrape off the whiskers of the man who rid this territory of Outlaw Bill Riley."

My sudden rise in notoriety was going to take some getting used to. "Well, put that way, I guess I can accept your kindness this one time." It was plain he wasn't going to budge.

He looked me up and down and wrinkled his nose. "First things first." Nattingwood showed me into a back room with a tin bathtub filled with clear water and an old kitchen stove where a big bucket steamed away. On an upended potato crate near the tub was a stack of water-wrinkled newspapers starting to turn brown with age.

"The water's clean. I just filled it up a few minutes ago. You're the first one in." He hefted the bucket from the stove and dumped the hot water into the tub. He set a second bucket on the stove and then cracked opened the back door to the alley behind the building to let out some of the heat and humidity. "Now you just take all the time you need." He closed the door to the shop behind him as he left.

I set my carbine and saddlebags in a corner, shed my six-shooter and clothes, and eased into the hot water. The heat instantly thawed my tense muscles. I lathered myself up and scrubbed away months' worth of grime.

Afterwards, I leaned back and grabbed a newspaper from somewhere out of the middle of the stack. It was an Omaha paper, and, from the date, it was more than eight months old. I'd been out of touch so long, even old news was a delight, and, anyway, for an eastern Missouri man like myself, any Omaha news was new news to me.

The big story of that day was the construction of a railroad bridge across the Missouri River to connect the UP with the C&NW. The ferry company complained it would put them out of business. Another story talked about finishing up the new Union Pacific headquarters in the old Herndon House Hotel building. Most of the stories seemed to touch on the transcontinental railroad one way or the other.

But not all. Six desperadoes had a shoot-out in Jefferson Square Park and murdered a city constable. Five of them ended up shot full of bullet holes, but the sixth, a fellow named Sherwin Turk, managed to escape and hightailed it up into the Dakota Territory. The sheriff was working with the territorial marshal in Yankton to get a posse together to go after him.

On page three was a short piece about how there were still no clues to the theft of a royal crown and something called "jewels of state" on their way to Sacramento to be put on display. Seems a prince-soon-to-be king by the name of Frederick, from some foreign land with a name I had a hard time pronouncing, had hired a private car to take him and his entourage on a buffalo hunt across the continent to the Pacific Ocean. All his stuff had gone missing when they'd transferred trains at Omaha. There was a pretty good woodcut picture of the baggage master looking mighty upset over the theft.

One article spoke of a recent county fair where a hotter-than-air balloon belonging to a professor had broken its tether in a high wind and went missing. Folks were still looking for it. The newspaper suspected both balloon and aeronaut, a man named Maurvelle, had perished in an accident. I got a chuckle out of a story about a bull elk that wandered into the brand new Coz-zens House Hotel and ran the guests outside into a winter blizzard.

All and all, it was uninspiring news and too old to be of any particular use. I set the paper back on the stack of papers and closed my eyes. The warm water would have soothed me to sleep if not for a nagging voice inside my head that kept intruding. Someone had stolen Bill Riley, and *I* was going to get him back, come brimstone fire or Missouri River flood!

Eventually I climbed out and dried myself. Afterwards, with the towel wrapped around my waist, I scrubbed my clothes and hung them to dry on a line sagging beneath the ceiling.

Wearing the towel, I barefooted it back to the main room and stepped up into the chair.

"You smell like a new man, Mr. Ragland," the barber declared, adjusting a striped apron about my neck.

"I feel like a new man."

"And you'll walk out of here *looking* like a new man as well." The barber's voice resonated like a finely tuned bass fiddle. He whipped up a fresh cup of shaving soap. "Clean skin, clean duds, and a clean chin."

I wanted to talk about the theft right off but decided that might not be wise. Instead I decided to work my way up to it,

54

to ask some questions first and get a feel for the town and its folks. Up until now Bend City had generally been a friendly place, except for that dirty rotten scoundrel who'd stolen Bill Riley. My anger lit a fire inside me again. Bill Riley had been more than simply a sizable investment of time and effort. The reward money would have finally convinced Pierre Toutant that I was worthy of Francine's hand; that I was capable of supporting his daughter.

I said, "It says on the window that you're a physician and a dentist, too."

"It's true. I began my studies in medical school, hoping to practice medicine in Poughkeepsie." He began lathering up my face.

"What happened to change your plans?" I asked him.

"The war happened."

"Oh. Well, I know how that is. So what brought you to the territory?"

The brush stopped and there was a long pause. "There are some questions one just doesn't ask, Mr. Ragland."

He was right. The territory was filled with men who for one reason or another felt the need to flee the States—the law, an ex-wife, an irate father. "Sorry. It's been a long trail," I offered as an excuse.

He accepted that as an apology and went on cheerfully, "No doubt, Mr. Ragland. Running the Riley gang to ground would not have been a Sunday picnic. Not a job I'd care to do."

In spite of everything, I managed to relax into the chair and close my eyes. The warm lather seeped into my pores and smelled like lime and rum. I'd been so long enduring the stench of Bill Riley's ripening head, the clean aroma was reinvigorating. But the feeling was fleeting. The theft was a weight on my chest I couldn't just put aside.

I said, "Seems Bend City is filled with people wanting to

leave." It was a safe enough subject. Sort of like commenting on the weather. And it touched on my investigation in that someone needing money to pull up roots would be the most likely to have robbed me.

"Oh, there are a few. Some people just naturally have itching feet. They'd want to move on even if they lived in a castle."

"You?"

The barber laughed. "I think about it from time to time. Not ready to act yet. I kind of like Bend City. Folks here are real friendly."

I decided to focus a little more sharply on the suspects at the top of my list. "Yep. That's the impression I had. Take those three gents at the card table last night. Toby McGill seems pleasant enough."

"McGill's a good man. Reliable as the coming of dawn every morning." The barber hesitated. "That is until he's had a few too many beers."

McGill, like everyone at the table, had been pretty oiled up by the end of the evening. "Oh?"

The barber lowered his voice. "Rumor has it McGill used to tend the stables down at Fort Garland in the Colorado Territory. The story goes he got liquored up one night, stole a string of army mounts, and traded them to the Utes for a pouch of gold nuggets. After he sobered up and realized what he'd done, he packed up his wagon, wife, and kids and skedaddled out of there. Headed north. Lost most of the gold through bad investments. Used what was left to build that livery stable down on Sawmill Road."

"Never would have guessed." I moved McGill to the top of my list of suspects.

"Like I said, it's only rumor."

"I'll keep that in mind." I steered the conversation to my next suspect. "The other man there, the young fellow who owns the café? He played his cards like he didn't have a whole lot to lose. I think he said he wanted to sell out and move on down the river."

The barber laughed, the razor skimming expertly across my chin. "Franklin Collins arrived about two years ago. He and his Margaret had pretty big plans. They must have thought Bend City was about to boom. Instead what they found was a town about to go bust."

"I sorta got the impression he found Bend City not to his liking."

"Not Franklin. He likes Bend City. Margaret's another story. She's used to warmer climes. That first winter she about froze to death. She was sneezing and coughing most of the season. Then come spring, the black flies about ate her to the bone. She finally gave Franklin an ultimatum. Either they're gone by fall, or she'll be leaving for St. Louis by herself. Well, fall is about here already. Franklin's been trying to find a buyer for his place. No takers. They're dead broke. The only way him and Margaret are getting to St. Louis is by shoe leather."

I pondered that a while and moved Franklin Collins up my list to the top, knocking McGill down a notch. "Reckon he was in the game to win a stake to get them down river."

"Likely true." The barber glided his razor smoothly along my cheek. "More likely he needed a few hours away from Margaret's carping."

I tried to put myself in Collins's shoes, with Margaret being Francine. My Francine would never be unreasonable like that—no, not my Francine.

The ring of the doorbell pulled my gaze off the embossed tin ceiling where I'd been watching a spider navigate the convolutions. Marshal Bulger came in and stared at me sitting there, her scum green eyes narrowing a little.

"I wondered about it, Mr. Ragland, but you've just answered

my question."

"What question was that?" I asked.

"Whether the crooks took your cash. But I see they left you with enough to buy a bath and a shave."

"They didn't take anything but the head and my army knife."

"And that answers another question," she said. "The thief wasn't one of the men at the table."

I didn't follow her logic. She must have seen I hadn't and said, "If he was, he'd have known about the cash in your pocket, having just lost to you."

"How did you know I won?"

She smiled. "I've already asked around about you, Mr. Ragland." She stood in front of me, slowly appraising me from my pink toes to my lathered face. "You've made quite a reputation for yourself in the short time you've been in Bend City."

I felt strangely flustered in Bulger's presence and didn't know why that should be. Something in her face; her eyes maybe? I said, "Well I . . . I'm pleased to see you're doing something about my stolen property."

"A crime has been committed in my town, and I intend to get to the . . . ahem"—her view shifted—"the bottom of it." She grinned and took a step toward the door but then looked back at me over her shoulder. "A piece of advice, Mr. Ragland. If you intend to go lounging around in a skirt, you ought to learn to sit like a lady."

It was an odd remark, and I cocked my head in dismay.

Her smile got larger, and I could have sworn she'd winked. "You're showing a bit more man flesh than is decorous," she said and left.

Startled, I sat up straight in the barber chair and tucked the towel down between my knees, my face suddenly afire.

The barber's sonorous laugh rumbled in the small shop. "That Bethany Bulger, she's a prize."

CHAPTER 7

Bethany Bulger was not a lady. She was coarse and vulgar, nothing at all like my sweet Francine. Marshal B. Bulger was not a person with whom I wished to become closely acquainted.

My face took on heat again remembering her brazen remark as I peeked out the barber shop door. I wasn't ready to confront the Marshal Bulger just yet. Checking that she was nowhere in sight, I hastened from the barber shop, wearing still-damp clothes, and turned into the café.

The place was deserted. Not even one customer at the counter. It was plain enough why Franklin Collins was barely making ends meet, and why he'd backed away from my offer last night like I'd been a rabid dog.

I sniffed the air for any sign of Bill Riley. Not a whiff of him. If he was here, he was sealed up tight somewhere. A table by the window gave me a clear view of the Buffalo Wallow Saloon across the street. Its doors were still closed, but then, it was early in the day. I waited a few minutes for Franklin to appear, read the handwritten menu to pass the time, and waited some more.

"Hello?" I called finally and listened for a response. I became aware of a scraping sound coming from somewhere out back behind the building, and the muffled sound of voices. They seemed to be arguing.

Curiosity drew me to the kitchen door, where a big pot sat upon the stove, curling steam toward the ceiling. Beyond it stood a shelf with some pots and pans and a couple rows of canned goods. It was a sparse pantry. Past that was a doorway to a weedy backyard. The voices were coming from there, louder now.

A woman was saying, "It's just another one of your harebrained schemes, Frank."

"Margaret, you know we're flat broke," Franklin said, trying to sound reasonable. "This is a way to change all that."

I moved closer to the door to better hear. It was probably none of my business, but then, maybe it was my business?

"And likely you'll be dead, and me a widow," she shot back. "Oh, Frank. You're so impulsive."

"Moving here and building this place, that's what you mean, don't you?"

"Not just this place." She sounded weary, as if this was not a new topic, but one they'd taken apart and put together more times than either cared to remember. "It was the greengrocer disaster in Omaha, and before that the bakery in St. Louis. And before that the garden nursery you wanted to start up. Who buys trees and flowers when they can grow them from seed free of charge?"

"I like trees and flowers . . . and vegetables," he said defensively. I envisioned a pout shaping his lips.

"I like vegetables, too." She sighed. "It's been one string of financial disasters after another. But at least each attempt was at something real."

"Businesses sometimes do good, and businesses sometimes fail. You know that as well as I." The words sounded old and worn out, as if he'd said them a thousand times before.

"Oh, Frank, I'll stick by your side in another attempt, if that's what it takes, but now this! I just don't know what you're thinking."

"*This* is a sure thing, Margaret. There is big money here."

"I got a bad feeling. It'll be another bust, only this time we won't simply walk away from it and start over. This time it'll bury you. You need to bury it here and now. Pretend you never heard a word of it. We can start over again somewhere else."

I'd heard enough. They were startled to see me come through the door. Franklin's face went pale. "Mr. Ragland! We were just talking about you."

They'd grown a vegetable garden here behind their place. The patch of ground near where he stood had been freshly turned. There were a few chickens in a coop and a goat tethered in the dry grass on the other side of a picket fence. The woman—Margaret—held a basket with some carrots, a bunch of scrawny onions, and a couple heads of cabbage.

Franklin said, "This is Mr. Ragland, Margaret. He's the man I told you about, the one who killed Bill Riley."

Her eyes widened with interest. "And you're lucky at cards, too, I hear," she said with the faintest hint of disapproval. She had a long, frowning face, straw-colored hair, and blue eyes. She'd spent too much time out in the sun. I thought about Francine; how she avoided the ravages of sunlight like a politician avoids the truth . . . I winced. That wasn't exactly the analogy I wanted to attach to my dear Francine.

I said, "I try not to make a habit of winning" and grinned.

She didn't seem to catch my little joke, so I had to explain it to her. "Last night Lady Luck chose to smile at me. She usually passes me by."

That brought a smile to her face, and suddenly she was pretty.

I eyed the freshly turned ground. "Doing some digging?" I'd not ask him straight out if he'd stolen Bill Riley. He'd have naturally said no, and that would have scared him off before I'd got a chance to put a net over his head.

Mrs. Collins indicated the vegetable basket in answer to my question. "I'm making vegetable soup, but it'll be a couple hours before it's ready."

I wasn't buying it. They were too nervous. Definitely hiding something.

Franklin glanced down at the shovel he was holding and set it aside with some other garden tools. "I didn't realize anyone had come in. I'll be right there to take your order, Mr. Ragland."

I said, "It's not like you've got a line of customers out the front door waiting on their breakfast."

Franklin gave a wry smile. "Unfortunately that's the way business goes here in Bend City."

"I only need a couple of eggs and some coffee." My stomach hadn't settled enough yet for anything heavier. Before going back inside, I gave that turned patch of ground another glance. It was something I intended to investigate—later.

The last person I wanted to see was waiting for me when I got back.

Well, maybe she hadn't been waiting for me, only waiting for someone to give a breakfast order to, but her face did catch a glow when I walked in from the kitchen.

"You cleaned up real good, Mr. Ragland," Marshal Bulger said, looking me up and down in a disturbing manner. Like a man—or woman—appraising a horse they were considering buying.

My face warmed again, but at least I was fully dressed this time. "Have you found the man who stole my property, Marshal Bulger?" My abruptness, I think, was simply self defense. I didn't want her to know that her earlier remark had embarrassed me.

Her pond-scum gaze narrowed a little, hardening. "It's been less than an hour since you reported the theft. I'm good, Mr. Ragland, but not *that* good."

I hitched a thumb over my shoulder at the kitchen doorway.

"Collins will be here directly. Or was it me you came looking for?"

"Given a choice between a man or breakfast, eggs and marmalade win out every time."

It was a good comeback, and maybe I *was* wearing my feelings a little too near the surface. Thinking it over, none of what had happened had been her fault. Maybe it was time to start over?

"I apologize for being rude, Marshal. It's just that I spent three hard months chasing down that killer. Losing him like I did . . . well, it sorta stings, if you get my meaning." That was as close to the truth as I could muster at the moment.

"I think I know what you mean . . . even if you don't. You're kicking yourself because you let liquor muddle your senses. You got drunk and careless, and now you need me to help you find what was taken from you. And maybe that grates a little, too, doesn't it? Me being a wisp of a woman and you being a big and husky man; kind of cuts at one's pride, doesn't it?"

I winced. "You're perceptive."

She smiled. "Some men just don't lie very well."

"I'll work on that."

"No, don't. A streak of honesty in a man is refreshing."

Franklin Collins came in at that moment, wiping his hands on a white apron that he'd put on somewhere between when I'd last seen him and now.

He seemed surprised and pleased to see the marshal. "Was just out back helping Margaret dig some vegetables. Your usual, Marshal?"

"Ruts can be comfortable places to be."

He looked at me inquiringly. "And eggs and coffee for you, Mr. Ragland?"

"Over easy. Some toast, too."

"I'll get right on it." Collins went back to the kitchen.

63

I looked at Marshal Bulger, suddenly at a loss for words. Standing there looking at each other felt sort of unnatural, so I motioned to the table by the window. "Would you care to join me, Marshal? We can talk out a plan for getting Mr. Bill Riley back."

"Don't know what kind of plan you're looking for, Mr. Ragland, but I'll listen to whatever ideas you have."

We sat across from each other, sunshine through the café's front window bright, warm, and lifting my spirits—a little. I still felt weak in the stomach, and suddenly very tired. Across the street the saloon remained buttoned up tight. I intended to speak with Bobby Parker just as soon as he opened those front doors for business.

In the strong light, Bethany Bulger looked older than I'd first suspected, and maybe a little wiser. Or maybe I was just getting used to her. Her eyes had changed some, too. Actually they were kind of attractive eyes, not exactly like pond scum, I admitted grudgingly. She wasn't exactly a pretty woman, but she might have been at one time.

Collins brought over cups of coffee, linen napkins, and silverware and went back to his kitchen.

I said, "Tell me about Franklin Collins, Toby McGill, and Henry Hagmann."

She gave me a patient, long-suffering smile. "Already told you it wasn't one of those three."

"How can you be sure?"

"For one, they left you with a pocketful of money."

"Small change compared to the bounty on Bill Riley." I tasted the coffee. It was weak, like Bobby Parker's watered-down whiskey.

She set her coffee cup back down on the table. "For two, they're not thieves."

"McGill stole army horses and sold them to the Injuns."

She rolled her eyes. "You've been listening to Boyd Natting-wood." She wagged a finger at me. "Repeat a rumor long enough, and small things get blown up all out of proportion to what really happened."

"Like me bushwhacking Riley and his partners and throwing their bodies in the river?"

She scowled. "That's how I heard it. Listen, this town is full of folk with skeletons in their closets, just like every other frontier town. People come out to the territories to get away from those skeletons. Take Toby McGill, for instance. Did he steal some army horses? Some might say he did, and some might say he was just taking matters into his own hands."

"That's a pretty liberal position for a lawman to take, Marshal. But then, you're not really a lawman, are you?"

"I'm not?" She sounded curious, not offended.

"I mean, your heart's not in it."

"Then why am I doing it?"

"You tell me."

Her lips tightened. I'd touched a tender spot, and she had no intention of revealing anything of a personal nature to me.

"All right," I said after shriveling under her stare for a moment. "Tell me why Toby McGill did or did not steal army mounts."

She brought her coffee cup to her lips, took a sip, and then set it down, her eyes never leaving my face. "You know, Mr. Ragland, I can't decide if you're just naturally annoying or if you're playing a game with me."

"Maybe it's that honest streak we talked about earlier?"

"Don't let it go to your head."

"McGill?"

"He worked for the army. Fort Garland. A civilian wrangler. The army didn't buy horses; they went out and caught them. Free-range animals. Most were barb horses, descendants of those brought up from Mexico a couple hundred years ago. They're short, powerful, and some are pretty good, once broken. Some aren't. McGill, he loved them all, tame or wild."

I saw where she was going with this. "But the army had no such feelings for the animals, I take it?"

She shook her head. "What you'd expect from a paper pusher, which is another name for military bigwig post commandant. He picked the best of the lot and ordered the others put down. McGill was appalled. He'd worked with those animals, groomed them, shoed them. He couldn't do it."

I'd only just met McGill, but that seemed a fair description of the man. "The barber said he sold them to the Utes."

"And that's just how rumors get out of hand, Mr. Ragland."

Franklin Collins arrived with our food and promised to be right back with more coffee.

Bethany turned her attention to the two poached eggs and piece of toast and began spreading marmalade. "What happened is, one evening after taps he took the horses out, telling the post guards he was moving them to some grass down by a seep a little way off.

"Soon as he got out of sight of the fort, he set about removing their halters. That's when the Utes showed up, curious as to what he was doing. The horses were green-broke and pretty tame, and, from the way McGill tells it, so were the Utes. The Indians liked the idea that the hard work was done and bartered with McGill to take the animals off his hands. Being a little drunk on account of what he'd been told to do, he agreed. There may have been some gold involved, but McGill never came out and admitted it."

Her explanation sounded reasonable, but it didn't convince me of McGill's innocence.

CHAPTER 8

We weren't exactly friends, standing on the sidewalk in front of the café after breakfast, but we had managed to sand down some of the rough spots. Our personalities were just too different. Fortunately all I needed from Marshal Bethany Bulger was a lead on who stole Bill Riley's head. I'd take it from there—her town or not—with or without her help.

Across the way the saloon's doors were still closed, while down the street my rented room called for me. A soft bed and feather pillow were what my weary bones wanted right now, but I sensed there was something else on Bethany Bulger's mind.

"You got plans, Mr. Ragland? I mean, right now?"

"Only to get some sleep. Hoping it might settle the buffalo stampede inside my head."

"There's something I'd like to show you." She hitched her head toward the tall hardware store at the edge of town. "It's not far from Mace's store."

We started down the sidewalk, the warm morning sun soaking deep into my shoulders feeling good. As our footsteps tapped out an easy pulse on the sidewalk planks, Bulger began to talk. "You wanted to know why I do it."

I said, "You seemed uneasy telling about it so I didn't press it."

She'd stopped a moment to look into a window at a display of bonnets. And then we walked on. "I appreciate the consideration, Mr. Ragland. I'm not one to pine for the past. When life up and takes a tumble, I don't talk about my trials to just anyone."

"You don't know me from Eve's better half."

She glanced at me and gave a short laugh. "If man's the better half, little wonder Eve took up with a snake."

A grin pushed at my face. "Had that coming. Why talk to me?"

"I wouldn't be, not if I'd let first impressions mean anything."

"I wasn't at my best when I showed up at your front door, was I?"

"You clean up okay, and you have manners. I was watching at the table. You asked a question, and after thinking it over I decided to give you an answer. Don't ask why. I'm not ready to look that deep."

We came to the corner of Bend Avenue and Sawmill Road and turned right, past a Chinese laundry and a clothing shop. An alleyway cut across Sawmill Road here, and the boardwalk ended. Only one building stood beyond the alley, an undertaker's parlor. Across the street from it in a weedy field stood a lone gray house with two windows flanking a gray door. In one window hung curtains of some flimsy material. The other window was bare, showing the building to be empty.

"That was Harel and Alice Lemuel's place," Bethany said, noting my interest. "They're gone."

"The couple who left by steamer the other day?"

She looked surprised that I knew of that.

"The warehouse clerk told me."

"Wert." She shook her head. "He's a strange one. Keeps to himself, keeps quiet, yet whenever I'm around him I have this distinct feeling there's a steam boiler inside that man about to burst."

The road climbed a slight hill, ending abruptly at a low, iron fence enclosing a rectangle of ground. We stopped at the cemetery gate. Beyond it a scattering of headstones marked the resting places of Bend City's former residents. The town was young, so it was no surprise the gravestones were few. Near the iron gate stood an ancient cottonwood tree. A long branch stretched out above the gate. I wondered briefly how the tree had managed to survive the woodsman's ax. Very little else around Bend City had, except for a patch of scraggly cottonwoods down by the river not far from Hagmann's Fishworks.

"Folks around here call it the hangman's tree."

"Convenient location," I noted wryly. "Anyone ever get hanged on it?"

Bethany Bulger laughed. "Local humor, Mr. Ragland, that's all it is. If we ever have need to hang someone, we'll build a proper gallows." The smile slowly faded from her face. She took in a breath and sighed. A sudden sadness had come over Bethany as I followed her through the gate into the graveyard. Except for the few groomed plots, it was mostly grassy prairie ground. In a far corner stood some tall stones. Not gravestones, just rocks that looked to have been set up in a little half-circle.

I suspected our reason for coming here, and when we stopped by one of the gravestones, I knew I'd been right. The name carved into the stone was *Brian Bulger. 1845–1871.*

"Your husband?"

"Brian had always wanted to be a deputy marshal. He was thrilled when he finally got an appointment from the territorial marshal. We moved up from Omaha." Her voice tightened. "Weren't in town but a month when the accident happened."

I was beginning to understand. "So you took over the job."

"Felt it was my responsibility. Now you know why I do it."

We stood there a while, quiet. I wondered why she showed me this part of her life. When I asked, she sighed and said simply, "In some ways you remind me of Brian." She didn't explain how I reminded her of him, and I didn't press the issue.

Bethany turned away from the grave and started for the black iron gate. I strolled quietly beside her. There weren't any words to say. As we left the cemetery I asked about the stones in the corner.

She seemed happy for the distraction. "They're old. Were here before the town was settled. Folks finally figured out that the stones marked an Indian burial mound, so when they fenced off Bend City Cemetery, they included it. Every now and again someone digs up Indian remains. When they do, the bones get reburied over in that corner."

"Is that where the ghosts come from?"

She gave me an odd look.

"The ones that scared the Lemuels out of town?" I glanced toward the abandoned house just outside the cemetery's iron fence.

Her eyes narrowed ever so slightly. "I suppose it might be, if you believe in such things."

From where I stood on the cemetery hill I had a wide view of the river. To the northeast the sky was clear. Not a smudge of smoke. Well, it wouldn't matter now. I wasn't about to board a steamer without Bill Riley.

Marshal Bulger walked with me as far as the corner and then said good-bye and turned up the street toward her office. I started for the hardware store.

"Whiskey?" The Injun had come out of nowhere and stood in my way with his begging hand out.

"You again?" With the wind coming just right, he reeked like a week-dead possum. Bill Riley had nothing over Chief when it came to pure, nasty stink. Bill smelled like a nosegay of magnolia flowers by comparison. I fanned the air and said, "Don't you have a teepee somewhere?"

"No teepee. Whiskey?"

"So you do understand English."

"Muy poquito."

"Spanish?"

"Oui."

"Huh?" My brain hurt too much to figure out what the crazy Injun meant. That knock to my head must have done more damage that I'd realized. I was getting real tired of bumping into Chief every time I turned around and told him to vamoose, pushing on toward the bed that waited for me.

I awoke to afternoon sunlight slanting through the window onto the foot of the rumpled bed. I'd slept hard right through the heat of the day. My body had plainly needed the rest. I swung my feet to the floor and sat there a while, feeling hungry again. That was a good sign. Rising cautiously from the bed, my head remained reasonably in place, and nothing in the room moved in an unexpected way. Another good sign. I went to the window. The street below was quiet and filling with evening shadows.

Someone knocked on the door. Wally Mace stood there when I opened it.

"I heard about the loss of your, ahem, dinner, Mr. Ragland."

I stepped back to let him into the room. "I imagine everyone in town's heard about it by now."

Mace said, "Not the sort of news a head-stealing thief would want to get around. I suspect he's buried Bill Riley somewhere far out of sight by now . . . in a manner of speaking." He smiled at his little joke, stroking his neatly trimmed beard.

"Unless he's already left town," I said ruefully.

Mace thought about that a moment. "Few folks come, and few go, and them that do go tend to make a production of it. You know, steamer trunks piled high on the wharf or in the back of a wagon." He gave a sly grin. "I suspect they do that to make those who have to stay envious."

"But they don't make you envious?"

"I like Bend City. Got a feeling it'll be here a long while."

"That's not the sort of feeling I'd bet hard money on, Mr. Mace. Old Man Missouri might have a thing or two to say about it."

"Oh, maybe someday he'll talk to these folks down at the sawmill and along the wharf, but he'd have to climb most of twenty feet to have a conversation with us up here along Bend Avenue." Mace smiled. "I don't think he's up to that. Bend City has possibilities. The river has possibilities. Location, location."

I wasn't so sure. I'd seen the Missouri shake itself awake from a long sleep and spread out like one of those Greek monsters of old. I didn't think a twenty-foot rise in elevation would be much of a challenge should he get it in his head to do some housecleaning. "Yours seems to be a singular opinion."

He shrugged. "Some men have vision. Others pull up roots and move on."

Move on? I felt a twinge of panic at the thought that Bill Riley might already be heading down river. "No riverboat arriving today?"

"No steamers today. Nor did anyone leave by wagon or horseback, far as I know."

I began to breathe a little easier. Mace moved on to the reason for his visit. "You staying another night?"

"I won't leave until I find what was stolen from me."

Mace's gray eyes gave off a greedy glint. "I have a feeling you'll be here a while then." He stuck out a hand.

I fished out a quarter and thumbed it into his palm. He left grinning, and I followed a few minutes later. Mace had said no riverboat had been by today. That meant the thief hadn't escaped that way. I felt pretty certain Bill Riley was still in town. I just didn't know where to look. Talking to Bobby Parker seemed a good place to start.

On my way down to the saloon, I swung by the stables to check up on Blue Shanks. I stepped through the big barn doors sniffing like a hound dog. All I smelled was manure and horse. Bill Riley's odor would be hard pressed to stand out here.

Blue Shanks was in her stall enjoying a bucket of oats. She turned her head and looked at me as I came up and stroked her neck. "Aren't you the contented gal." I checked her over. Her hooves had been trimmed, her mane combed, and her coat curried. McGill really did take care of his animals.

I went looking for the stableman. I found him out back shoveling manure onto a mound.

"Oh, hey, Mr. Ragland." McGill leaned on the shovel. "Some rotten luck, huh? Sorry to hear it."

"Some good-for-naught will be even sorrier when I find him," I said patting the Remington on my hip in a meaningful way.

McGill's view slid briefly toward the revolver, and his smile widened out. "Marshal Bulger will have a conniption."

"I've already informed the marshal. She knows my intent. Maybe it'll light a fire under her to find the fellow before I do."

"Good luck with that." He laughed. "If it were me who stole that head, I'd find someplace to stash it and wait you out. You've got a long hill to climb, I'm afraid."

McGill was right, but I've climbed hills before, and Bend City wasn't all that big a place. "If you were to hazard a guess, Mr. McGill, who here in town might have stole Mr. Riley?"

"I wouldn't hazard such a guess, Mr. Ragland. Truth is, don't know of anyone here who'd do such a thing."

I watched his eyes as he talked. The eyes are the first to give away a man telling a lie.

"I know most everyone hereabouts. About half of 'em would look at your Mr. Riley as their ticket outta here, including me. But far as I know, none of 'em are thieves"—his eyes narrowed—"including me."

I figured now wasn't the time to bring up his dealings with those army mounts. I needed to keep folks friendly or they'd all hunker down like a cork in a bottle, and I'd get nowhere. Anyway, McGill had showed no sign of lying, unless he was a very good liar. It was time to turn a corner on this conversation. "Blue Shanks looks happy as a pig in a wallow."

"That's the thing about animals, Mr. Ragland. When they're content they show it, and when they're unhappy, they show that, too. They're just plain honest folk. You never have to guess what they're feeling. Too bad humans aren't so easy to read."

That pinched a little, like maybe it had been pointed at me? Maybe he'd figured out that I'd made a list of suspects, and that his name appeared prominently on it? I played innocent. "Blue Shanks has lots of good qualities. Mostly she listens to me gripe and doesn't talk back."

He grinned. "Not too many women you can say that about, Mr. Ragland."

We chatted a while about the weather, the mosquitoes, the Injuns moving in, and the white folk moving out. I mentioned the mule over at the warehouse, and he said he'd already looked at the split hoof, but Wert figured it would heal okay if left alone.

McGill walked me back out through the barn, and as we passed by Blue Shanks he peeked in on her grub. Then we stood outside the big doors looking up Sawmill Road, now filled with shadows. The distant graveyard was a dusky smudge under the spread of that big old cottonwood tree. I offered to advance him on the board, but he said he'd tally it up when I was ready to leave town.

As I was about to go on my way, I asked if he'd seen anyone leave town today. He shook his head. "I board most of the saddle mounts and teams in town except for Hagmann's and Wert's, and one or two others. None left their stall today. But if someone does leave town, I'll keep my eyes . . . and nose . . . open for you. I hope you find your bounty head."

We said good-bye, and I pointed my boots up to Bend Avenue and then toward the Buffalo Wallow Saloon. It was hard to finger McGill as the thief. He came off as being genuine, but no one was above suspicion. He could have hidden Bill Riley anywhere, and I'd never know it from the smell of the place. Maybe even under that pile of manure he'd been building when I'd come in?

No one had left Bend City by horseback or steamboat today. Other than by keelboat or pirogue, that left only one other way out of town—Shanks' mare.

CHAPTER 9

I didn't run into Chief, and that was just fine by me, but as I neared the saloon the memory of last night's encounter with Parker's whiskey started my stomach to churning. I made my way past the usual assortment of Injuns hanging around and peered over the batwing doors into the smoky saloon. Parker was hunched over the bar reading a newspaper. Only a couple of men were inside, not enough business to keep him occupied. Nothing like the flurry of business last night with Bill Riley drawing men in off the street. Peering into the saloon now, my stomach began to cramp. I decided to postpone going inside.

Instead, I strolled down to the wharf to check out the traffic down there. Those same two boats from the day before were still tied to the long pier. On the other side of the pier, Henry Hagmann's small fishing fleet had come into dock, and his war party of Cheyenne fishermen were busy unloading the day's catch into hand carts and wheeling them into the cannery.

Just then the warehouse clerk emerged from the big building, locking the door behind him, and started along the wharf toward the sawmill. He looked over, startled, when I fell in step beside him.

"Much traffic on the river today?" I asked casually.

His big shoulders hunched forward, and he shifted his view to the ground. "No steamer today. Maybe tomorrow."

I said, "Heard it's been pretty quiet along the river today."

"You heard right." He hurried on, plainly not wishing to

make small talk.

I bade him a good evening and watched him plod on his way and turn the corner onto Sawmill Road, where McGill's corrals ran alongside the street.

No steamers. No riders. Not a single boatman. Bill Riley had to still be in town. As I stood there near the little corral, the mule drifted on over and stuck his nose through the rail.

Wert hadn't mentioned Bill Riley. Had he not yet heard about the theft? That was unlikely, seeing as how news spreads like measles through a small place like Bend City. I scratched the mule's soft, gray muzzle and said, "You've an unfriendly owner, I regret to say. He's a queer fellow for sure. What sort of man would let a handsome animal like you suffer with a split hoof and not tend to it in a proper fashion?" I stopped talking and made a wry smile. Here I was again, talking to hoofstock like it was a real person.

I strolled out onto the nearest pier. The sun was setting, and the river lay like a dark ribbon, its waters slowly moving ever southward. Someplace far away it would marry up with the Mississippi and then eventually spill out into the Gulf of Mexico.

My journey would not take me that far. After Fort Leavenworth I'd flee to St. Louis, where Francine's open arms waited for me. The thought of her there and me here laid a heaviness upon my chest somewhere near my heart.

I didn't notice the mosquitoes and black flies until I slapped my neck and then my cheek. Tiny bloody smears appeared on my hand. In a rush they descended out of nowhere and began eating me up! Right then I figured Mrs. Collins to be one of the more sensible citizens of Bend City for wanting to leave. I'd be gone in a blink if not for Bill Riley. Thinking of Margaret Collins reminded me of what needed to be done tonight.

As I started back into town, my view swept along the dark riverbank and stopped upon the flicker of a distance campfire amongst the lone stand of cottonwood trees at the water's edge. A vagabond's camp, by the look of it. I wondered how the folks down there were managing the mosquitoes. Probably no better than me.

Trudging up the hill into town, it occurred to me a campsite along the river would be a likely place for a thief to hide out. I stopped, thinking I ought to investigate the matter, but the hordes of mosquitoes persuaded me otherwise. The voracious vermin, it seems, had sent smoke signals to their kin about this warm-blooded feast standing right there in the middle of their territory.

I would check out that riverside camp in the morning, I told myself, hurrying away from the vicious black swarms.

Lingering about the corner of Bend and River, slapping mosquitoes and trying to be inconspicuous, I watched the men outside the saloon, not recognizing anyone from the night before. That meant nothing. There'd been a lot of faces, and I was a newcomer to Bend City.

The saloon was mostly empty—a good time to question Bobby Parker. As much as I wanted to, I put it off. The memory of last night still had my stomach queasy and turning knots. I hadn't done anything about my hunger yet, and maybe that was part of the problem. The Big Muddy Café still showed lights through its window, so I crossed the street to correct the matter.

Like the saloon, business here was dismal. Four people. A man and woman at one table, a gent at the eating counter. I took the table in the corner that I'd occupied yesterday.

Franklin Collins spied me soon as I came through the door and beat a path like I'd been a long lost brother . . . from the wealthy side of the family.

"Did you find Bill Riley?" he asked hopefully.

"I'm on his trail," I said, stretching the truth a long mile.

Franklin wasn't really listening. He had something on his mind, about to burst a seam to let it out. "Can I ask you something?"

I nodded, a bit wary at all his enthusiasm.

"I'll be back in a trice." He dashed off through the back door into the kitchen, returning a few seconds later with a roll of paper. Pushing aside the salt and pepper shakers, Franklin spread a map of the Dakota Territory on the table in front of me.

Upon it were sketched out a few prominent features, some named, some not. A few squiggly lines depicted rivers—more or less in their approximate locations. The larger rivers had been identified by name, as had a couple of the settlements along the Missouri River. I'd seen another map like it back at Fort Leavenworth, but this one was different. Someone had drawn in more details, more than even I was aware of—especially in the area of the Black Hills, what the Sioux call the Paha Sapa.

I looked up at him. "Where'd you get this?"

"A couple months ago an old timer by the name of Carson Grove was through here. He was a buffalo hunter for the railroad and now hunts meat for the army. He had interesting stories to tell. He marked some details on this map."

I studied it. It looked to be an accurate rendering of the places I'd recently traveled. "You fixing on making a journey?"

"Me? No!" he said quickly. "I . . . I, er, was just remembering your telling of how you tracked down the Riley Gang. I wonder if you could show me how it went. If you wouldn't mind?"

"Why?"

He smiled the smile a fox. "I found the story fascinating."

I thought the request strange. Franklin had something going on he didn't want to tell me, but I couldn't see any harm in recounting the chase. I started where I'd picked up their trail, running a finger to where they'd murdered the homesteader and his wife, and then to where I lost them. "Picked them up here," I said, tracing the place where I made my Cheyenne River crossing, "and ended it about here in the Paha Sapa." My finger came to rest on the prominent feature toward the bottom left corner of the map.

He stared at it a long moment and cleared his throat. "Er, you said you caught them down by a river?" he asked kind of timidly. "Where might that have been?"

"It wasn't really a river. More like a no-name creek." I studied the map again. "I'm thinking it's this one here. It comes out of the hills about here and finds the Belle Fourche right there. Looks like your friend Carson Grove sketched it out pretty good."

Franklin Collins was in a chipper mood after that, rolling up his map and coming back a little later with a cup of coffee and a bowl of Margaret's vegetable soup. When I went to pay him, he wouldn't take my money, claiming I was a special guest and that the meal was on the house.

Franklin and Margaret could little afford giving away food, but arguing the matter with him would have got me no further than it had with the barber this morning. I hadn't got used to being a celebrity yet. Probably never would. All this notoriety made me itchy under the collar and even more anxious to be on my way down river.

Later, with my stomach comfortably full, I took a chair on the boardwalk outside the druggist store, across the street from the saloon and kitty-corner from the café. The mosquitoes weren't bad now, as the air had turned cool. A fine mist hovered over the river below, highlighted by the thin moonlight. I leaned back and closed my eyes.

I must have dozed. When I woke, the Big Muddy Café's window was dark, and so were the two windows on the floor above it where Franklin and Margaret lived. Voices spilled from the saloons on the other side of the street. I wondered in a distracted way how much watered-down whiskey Bobby Parker had left to sell, seeing as fresh stock hadn't arrived by river today. My stomach still didn't feel like finding out.

By where the sliver of moon in the cloudless sky stood, I reckoned the hour to be near midnight. The moon didn't cast too much light. It was a good night for the business I had in mind. I strolled toward the edge of town, and soon the brittle prairie grass rustled under my boots. In the dark I circled wide and came to the picket fence behind the Big Muddy Café. I could still hear the sounds of voices from the saloon across the street, but now they were muffled by the building between us.

I felt in the dark for the latch, the gate opened quietly, and I slipped into Franklin and Margaret's vegetable garden. The chickens in their coop clucked softly; the goat moved back to the corner of his little pen and watched me creep past. The crickets had gone silent at my approach. They started chirping again.

A distant dry rustling brought me to a stop alongside the little tool shed. A pair of green eyes out on the prairie watched me. Coyote. I let go of a breath but remained where I was until the critter moved off.

Quietly lifting the shovel from where Franklin had earlier leaned it, I pushed it into the newly turned soil more or less where he'd been digging that morning. It went in easy. I worked quietly so as not to wake the sleeping occupants in the building a few yards away. About eight inches down the point of the shovel thumped against a piece of wood, giving an encouragingly hollow sound. My heart beat faster as I hurriedly removed the topsoil. Down on hands and knees I brushed the dirt off the lid to a buried box.

And then the crickets went silent.

I was all but invisible there hunkered down in the shadows,

so I stayed that way, only my eyes searching. I can be as patient as a cat at a mouse hole, but after a while my hunched-over position began to make itself known in my back and shoulders.

A foul odor, something akin to stale urine, drifted past on the light river breeze. It made me think of Hagmann's fish shack.

After a minute the odor passed by, and crickets took to fiddling again. I eased out of my frozen stance and quickly dragged the rest of the dirt off the top of the buried box. My fingers found a rope handle and, giving a tug, the lid came away.

There wasn't much depth to the box. Feeling carefully inside, I determined it was filled with sand . . . and something else, too. Something like hair poked through the sand. Grabbing a handful of it, a hard tug pulled it free. I lay there on my stomach staring at a bunch of carrots!

I'd uncovered Franklin Collins's makeshift root cellar.

CHAPTER 10

The blare of a steam whistle jolted me straight up in bed, squinting in the bright morning light filling the window. I'd slept later than I'd planned. I must have been more exhausted than I'd thought, and now the day was well along, and worse yet, a steamboat had arrived!

The hard, crisp sound of the steam whistle floated up from the river again. Was the boat arriving or departing? Had Bill Riley made his escape?

I bolted out of bed, into my clothes, out the door, and down the staircase.

Wally Mace was waiting for me on the sidewalk at the bottom of the stairs. "Missed you yesterday," he said.

"A steamer's arriving," I said attempting to push past him.

But he was quick on his feet, and he blocked my dodge. "Oddly enough, they do that from time to time." He grinned and stretched out an upturned palm. "Twenty-five cents for last night. Make it fifty if you plan on sleeping here tonight."

I didn't have time for Mace's pleasantries. I pressed two quarters into his greedy palm and dashed off down Sawmill Road, past the livery, and out onto the wharf.

The steamer was coming upriver, not heading down. A burden lifted from my shoulders. Anyone fixing to cash in on Bill Riley would have to travel downriver to Fort Leavenworth. This was a small, flat-bottom packet with a single paddle out back and two tall chimneys forward amidships, furiously pumping gray smoke into the blue morning sky. The packet had been painted bright white at one time, but that time had been long ago, as most of the paint had flaked off, revealing grayish wood beneath. The sorry looking creature appeared to have been rode hard and put away wet all its life.

Missouri riverboats were not generally long lived to begin with, what with snags and sawyers, fires and Injun attacks, and the most feared of all—boiler explosions.

As I stood there watching, the packet turned shoreward and slowed to a drift that neatly put it alongside the nearer of the two piers. Whoever was behind the helm was an expert pilot. Hawsers were tossed and secured, and strong black arms pulled the boat to the fenders. The name *De Witt* was painted in flaking red paint across the front of the pilot house. A *Benton Line* "P" banner fluttered from a wire stretched between the chimneys.

I joined the crowd gathering near the pier—mostly business-men, wood hawkers . . . and the just plain curious. I reckon I fell into that latter group, although my curiosity had a purpose. My nose was busy searching for telltale odors of Bill Riley's presence. The only odor I smelled was of salted fish from Henry Hagmann's Fishworks.

"She's headed the wrong direction for you, Mr. Ragland," a gruff voice said beside me. I turned. The burly warehouse clerk squinted at me against the sunlight.

"Just as well," I said, "as I'm not ready to shuck off Bend City just yet."

The clerk nodded knowingly. "Yes, yes, the stolen head."

So he'd finally heard. I said, "You wouldn't know anything about it now, would you?"

"Me?" He seemed shocked I would even think that of him and looked away. "I try not to know anything that's none of my business."

A gang of stevedores heaved out the gangplank and set it

securely in place on the pier. The clerk glanced at a clipboard in his hand and hurried away like a little boy caught filching a lemon stick, I thought suspiciously. Well, his departure really wasn't all that strange. At the moment everyone was guilty in my eyes, even . . .

Bethany Bulger?

The marshal appeared from around the corner of Hagmann's Fishworks and stood just beyond the edge of the crowd, looking about.

The purser, with a dead-letter packet slung over his shoulder, tromped across the gangplank, weaving his way through the gathering crowd. He parked himself in the middle of the wharf and began calling out names from a list, but he wasn't having much luck finding owners to lost mail. I only half heard him as I watched Bethany, craning her neck this way and that, standing on her toes, moving a few steps this way and then a few steps that way.

And then suddenly her view shot like an Injun arrow straight for the gangplank. Two men wearing rumpled black suits and carrying valises emerged from the shadows of the boat's boiler deck. Presently they debarked and made their way down the pier.

I backed up alongside a freight cart, behind a pile of wooden boxes. Marshal Bulger moved, too, nearly vanishing behind the rows of cordwood stacked along the edge of the wharf. Her gaze remained on the two men as they paused on the pier, glancing about. Finally they aimed their steps at River Street and trudged out of sight around the corner heading up into town.

As I watched them leave, movement caught the corner of my eye and pulled it toward the row of buildings along the wharf. Someone stood in the dark gap between the Murry & Murry Territorial Transfer Bank and a ship's chandler shop. The someone moved from the shadows to the edge of the building, where sunlight caught the greasy gleam of long hair, a grimy wool vest, red shirt, buckskin britches, and cheap glass beads.

Chief.

He hadn't seen me, and he wasn't begging whiskey money either. He looked stone sober, his view fixed upon Marshal Bethany Bulger. She left the cordwood stack and followed the strangers into town. Once out of sight, Chief emerged from the gap, looked at the steamer a long moment, and then set off after the marshal.

I waited behind the boxes another minute to see if anyone else was interested in joining the parade. No one appeared to be. I moved out to trail after all four of them when Bobby Parker and another gent came down the road pulling an old Mormon handcart.

I'd been wanting to talk to Parker a while now, and this was a good opportunity to do so. Whatever business the marshal had with those two men in the rumpled suits wasn't any business of mine. Chief, on the other hand, had got my curiosity up, but he could wait. Talking to Parker was more important at the moment.

They hauled the cart out onto the wharf, down the pier, and stopped near the gangplank. Parker said something to the man, leaving him to watch the cart while he boarded the boat.

Pushing through the crowd, I strolled out onto the pier and stopped near the handcart. "Mr. Parker's whiskey finally came in?"

The man leaning against the cart turned his head toward me. "Bobby's hoping so. He's gone aboard to check." He looked at me closer. "You're Mr. Ragland, aren't you?"

I scratched the back of my neck and grinned. "Guess I've achieved some notoriety here in Bend City."

"Not every day a famous gunman comes to town."

"I'm not all that famous," I said, trying to sound humble.

"I meant Bill Riley," he said, and then realized how that must have sounded and scrambled to cover his tracks. "Not that you aren't famous, too, Mr. Ragland. I mean anyone who can track down and bushwhack the Riley gang, and then skin the hides off ever' one of them thieving, murdering outlaws is a mighty brave man in my book. Yessiree, mighty brave."

"I didn't bushwhack Riley, nor did I skin anyone." Where were folks getting this nonsense? "Riley drew down on me first."

His eyes got big as chestnuts. "Well that proves what a fearsome gunman you are, shooting it out with six desperadoes like that."

"There were only three," I said, but I don't think he heard. Like Marshal Bulger, he had the story in his head the way he wanted to believe it, and that was good enough for him. I needed to find Bill Riley and get myself out of Bend City before the story got any bigger. Soon they'll have me shooting it out with General Custer's Seventh Cavalry!

Bobby Parker clumped across the gangplank scowling. "It come in. All ten barrels. But the captain won't take a letter of credit. He wants cash." Parker spied me, and his scowl darkened. "Figured you left town."

"Still got business here."

Parker nodded understandingly. "I wish you luck with your 'business.' Maybe you should have sold Mr. Riley to me like I offered? Now you gotta hunt down the criminal. It could be anyone."

"Hunting down criminals is what I do," I said with forced bravado. Him reminding me of that chafed a little.

Parker turned away, dismissing me and the discussion, and his face scrunched up in deep thought. He said to the fellow with him, "I got an idea. I'll be right back" and hurried off across the wharf toward the Territorial Transfer Bank.

"What's that about?" I asked.

The fellow shrugged. "I'm just hired help."

I waited by the cart with him, watching the bustle of crates being off-loaded and barrels of salted fish being carried aboard. The purser finished his mail call duty and carried the packet of dead letters back aboard the steamer. A couple of gents disembarked and wandered up into town. Those few men from town who went aboard must have been conducting business of some sort. None carried luggage or anything else that might have hidden a head. Men stood about smoking cigars, talking business and news from down in the States, politics, and the weather. Money changed hands. Amongst all this activity, four stevedores were busily hauling firewood aboard the *De Witt,* stacking it on the main deck near the fireboxes.

"Lived in Bend City long?" I asked Parker's helper just to make talk.

He gave a quiet laugh and shook his head. "Nobody's lived in Bend City very long."

"Why do you suppose that is?"

He thought it over. "Because Bend City is just a stopover for most folks heading somewhere else, or a place to wait out trouble till it blows over back wherever they come from."

"Yep, that's the feeling I get, too," I said, watching Irwin Wert hitch his mule to a flatbed cart and lead it across the wharf, the poor animal favoring its hoof. Two stevedores helped Wert heft a heavy crate onto the cart, and they all moved to the big warehouse door and disappeared inside. A minute or two later the stevedores emerged from the big building and returned to the *De Witt.*

And then Bobby Parker strode across the wharf, a wide look of accomplishment on his face. "Got me a loan," he said, pausing a moment by the cart before pointing his steps at the wide plank that bridged the chasm of dark water.

A question came to mind. I said, "Is Mr. Parker a gambling man?"

"Bobby? Naw, not Bobby. He don't spend a penny unless it will earn him two back."

I thought about that. The sound of footsteps pulled my view back to the gangplank. Three stevedores had appeared from the bowels of the riverboat, each with an oak barrel on his shoulder. Going back and forth, they quickly filled the handcart. Those barrels that wouldn't fit in the cart were set along the edge of the pier.

Parker's helper, a man I later learned was named Grimes, took the hand pulls while Parker leaned into the cart from behind. I fell in alongside him to give them a hand pushing the cart. The load was heavy, and the dry axle creaked as we trundled off the pier and started up the road.

I'd played coy long enough, so I came right to the point. "You know most of those men who were there that night who'd seen Bill Riley, don't you?"

Between grunts, Parker said, "Think one of them stole him?"

I was grunting, too, under the load. "Who else would have known?"

He managed a laugh. "About ever'one in town. Word gets around."

That was true, but I was trying not to let facts get in the way of my beliefs. "It might have been someone else, but my money's riding on it being someone who was in the saloon that night. Let's just suppose it was one of 'em. Who would you suspect?"

He snorted. "Half the men here in town are on the run. That's why they come out to the territories."

"The other half?"

He glanced at me, his face scrunched under the strain of pushing the cart. "No more brains than a tadpole, or they wouldn't have come in the first place. And that includes me. A few folks have seen the light and packed out. Most of us would if we could afford to leave. Some have too much invested— McGill and Collins, for example. Neither one can afford to up and leave. They've sunk everything they own into Bend City, and it's not likely they'll find someone to buy them out." He gave a long grunt as the road steepened, sweat beading on his forehead, heels digging in. "Except maybe Mace. He seems to have grand expectations for Bend City."

As far as I knew, Wally Mace hadn't been there that night. I said, "Mace seems to be doing okay."

"He makes out, but I think Mace arrived here with a pocketful of money."

I couldn't see how that would figure into my problem, but I tucked it away in the back of my brain anyway. "And Hagmann?" The road leveled out, and Parker and I started breathing a little easier. Grimes steered the cart into an alleyway behind the saloon near where a pile of empty whiskey barrels lay off to one side.

Parker's eyes shifted toward me, narrowing down some. "Hagmann. Hmm. I didn't think about him. He's a shrewd one. He managed to get the Cheyenne to work for him cheap and then did a shrewd contract with the government to ship provisions upriver to Fort Sully."

"Those barrels of salted fish being loaded aboard the *De Witt*?"

"Some go upriver to the forts, and some go down to the City of Kansas and the railway there."

The handcart creaked to a halt by the back door of the saloon. We leaned against the tailgate, breathing hard and slinging sweat from our brows. I said, "Hagmann and Mace are set up pretty good here. They aren't going anywhere. And neither are you."

His head came about, his eyes showing surprise. "Where did

you get an idea like that?"

"You've got the only saloon in town," I noted.

He huffed. "I'd be outta here lickety-split if I didn't own this boat anchor." He hooked a thumb toward the back door and, shaking his head, went around and opened it.

We hauled the barrels inside a storeroom and stacked them on a rack against the wall, beneath a shelf holding a couple dozen empty whiskey bottles. The bottles displayed all sorts of different labels, but I had a suspicion each one would be filled from the same cask. Parker was pretty particular how he wanted the casks arranged, the whiskey on one end of a rack and the beer on the other. A barrel with a brass faucet tapped into the bunghole lay on its side atop a makeshift stand, and another cask stood in a corner sort of out of the way.

Fresh sawdust covered the floor, and the makings of a box of some sort sat on a pair of sawhorses in the middle of the little storeroom. A hammer, saw, and a keg of Wally Mace's nails lay alongside it. Parker acted as if it wasn't there, and he ignored my curiosity when I took a closer look.

We returned to the wharf for the rest of the whiskey and beer, and afterwards, as a way of showing his appreciation for our help, Parker invited me and Grimes to a table for a drink on the house before opening the saloon for business. The whiskey was of the same watered-down stock from before, not the fresh lot we'd just hauled in, but my stomach had seen enough time to recover from its first encounter with the stuff, so I accepted his offer.

Grimes had heard Parker and me talking on the way up the hill and said, "Have you considered the Injuns? They would have heard about Riley and the reward. They sometimes act a little unaware, but they ain't really. They're always looking for a way to make a dime, especially after they've acquired a taste for whiskey."

I gave Grimes a surprised look. "Hadn't thought about that."
Parker said, "How would an Indian collect the reward?"
Grimes shrugged. "I don't know shucks about going after
bounty money but seems to me it's not writ down nowhere that
you gotta be a white man to ride the bounty trail. I heard plenty
of Mexicans are doing it down south of here."

Parker looked at me. "What about that, Mr. Ragland?"

Grimes's suggestion made sense. I said, "I'd never heard of
an Injun bounty hunter before but don't see why it wouldn't be
possible. I reckon the authorities over at Fort Leavenworth
wouldn't be too particular who brought Bill Riley in."

I got to thinking about Chief and the interest he seemed to
have taken in me. I'd assumed it was because he saw me as an
easy mark for his next drink. But maybe not. Maybe he'd known
all along about Bill Riley.

CHAPTER 11

Grimes's notion that an Injun might have taken Bill Riley had stirred up a beehive of worry inside me. I was on the lookout for Chief, but now that I wanted to find him, he was nowhere to be found. As the hours passed, my worry grew from a little cloud on the horizon to a big, black, ugly thunderhead. I'd convinced myself Grimes was correct. I imagined Chief having already slipped out of town with Bill Riley, even now making his way down river for Fort Leavenworth.

I stopped by the livery to inquire of any comings or goings—mostly goings—and to check in on Blue Shanks. She stood in her stall, slack-hipped and looking contentedly lazy. McGill wasn't in the barn, so I wandered out back where a dozen or so horses stood about the long corrals, batting flies with their tails. McGill wasn't here either.

Turning back to the barn, my view halted on that pile of manure he'd been building the other day. A suspicious scowl creased my forehead. A person might hide an odoriferous thing like Bill Riley's head under all that manure, and no one would ever know. It was kind of a crazy notion, but it had got in my head. A shovel leaned against a rail nearby, and no one was around. I glanced about. It was just me and some horses and the great big pile of sh—

"Hello, Mr. Ragland." McGill came around the corner of the barn hitching an arm through his suspender strap. I stared at him a little guiltily, but I don't think he noticed. "Looking for me? I was just out back seeing an Indian about a blanket."

"Which Injun?"

McGill grinned. "The privy, Mr. Ragland. The privy."

"I knew that," I said, feeling foolish. Chief was so heavy on my mind, I wasn't thinking straight, nor was I in a humorous mood. "Talking about Injuns, you haven't seen one wandering about today wearing a dirty, red shirt and glass beads around his neck?"

"Well now, I believe you've just described half the Indians in Bend City."

"He stinks like buffalo piss," I added, hoping to narrow it down some.

McGill laughed. "And that, Mr. Ragland, pretty much describes the other half."

I left there knowing I'd not made a favorable impression on Mr. McGill. Well, I'd had things pressing on my mind, I consoled myself, making an excuse for my awkwardness. McGill had told me one important bit of news. No mounts or other conveyances had departed his stable so far today.

I made my way up Bend Avenue. There seemed to be a lot more Injuns about, now that I was actually paying attention to them. I wasn't so sure they didn't outnumber the white folk. But no sign of Chief.

I was scanning the sidewalk across the street when my view passed over the marshal's office window. Beyond gray curtains that had been tied back to let in the sunlight stood Marshal Bulger and those two rumpled-suited gents from off the steamer this morning.

I'm not sure why that drew my attention, except that Chief had taken a peculiar interest in them, too. There'd been something different about Chief this morning. He'd been sober for one thing, and focused for another. It was a puzzle. Thinking it over, I suddenly wasn't at all convinced that Chief had lit a shuck for Fort Leavenworth with Bill Riley after all.

I changed the manner of my searching and began probing the shadowy gaps between the buildings and scanning the upper porches of those few buildings along Bend Avenue that, like the hardware store, rose more than one story high. There weren't but three of them.

I didn't spy Chief right off, but I was a hunter, and I had patience. I leaned against the wall of the millinery shop where I'd stopped and made a slow sweep of the town. There was no sign of Chief from this angle, so I crossed over to the other side of the street to the sidewalk in front of the bank building and started over again.

And there he was. A smile eased across my face as a great weight of worry lifted from my chest. Chief hadn't run off with Bill Riley after all. He'd hunkered himself down atop the roof of Macklin's Dry Goods and Clothing store, behind the facade, where he had a clear sight of the marshal's office and the two gents inside. From where I stood, only the brim of his tattered hat showed, and once in a while a corner of his cheek.

What was it about those two that had caught Chief's eye? Maybe they looked prosperous enough to buy him more whiskey? Whatever it was, it had no bearing on my problem, so I let it be and went about the business of searching for Bill Riley.

With no clear plan anymore, the only thing I knew for sure was that, unless he'd been buried, the smell of him would give away his location sooner or later. I started on one end of the street and visited every shop and tried every closed door.

By nightfall I'd managed to snoop through most the buildings in town and the alleyways, too, all the while my nose working the air like a rat in a scullery. I had encountered some curious odors, but none matching that of a human head weeks past planting time.

Another night came on. There was only one place left I hadn't yet checked out. That place would require breaking and entering and needed to be done when no one was around, which meant after the Buffalo Wallow Saloon closed up for the night. As long as Bobby Parker kept pouring whiskey, there'd be men out and about and near the place where I had business to tend to.

Seeing as I had a while to wait, I headed back to my room to catch a few hours' sleep.

I climbed the outside stairs to the second-floor door of Wally Mace's hardware store and opened it to the long hallway stretching out like a black tunnel in front of me. A hint of night glow came through a small window at the far end of the hallway. A dim, yellow streak seeped under one of the doors.

Two steps into the hallway, my feet stopped, and I stood there staring.

The pencil line of light was coming from under the door to my room. My first thought was that Mace had rented it to someone else. But no; I'd paid him for tonight's rent this morning. My second thought was that Bill Riley had kinfolk who'd trailed me, seeking revenge. Easing the Remington from its holster, I sidled quietly up to the door and listened a long moment. All was silent on the other side except for an occasional *click, click,* like maybe someone moving checkers around a board.

Feeling tight as a clock spring, I slowly turned the doorknob and slammed it open, rotating quickly into the room, crouched low, pointing the Remington.

Sitting in the chair under a lamp that hung from the wall, Marshal Bulger looked up from the ball of yarn on her lap and the knitting needles in her fingers. She rolled her eyes. "Mr. Mace won't approve of having his door hinges sprung."

"What are you doing here?"

96

"That can't be a comfortable position, Mr. Ragland."

I stood out of my crouch and looked around the room. She was alone. My rifle still leaned in the corner where I'd left it, and my saddlebags still lay upon the bed. Both appeared untouched.

"Waiting," she answered at last.

"For me?"

"No . . . Pocahontas. But you'll do for now."

"Why?" I glared into her scummy eyes, although in truth I couldn't really see the color in the dim light.

She broke off the staring showdown first and glanced at the revolver in my hand. "I've no doubt you're mighty good with that thing, having bushwhacked the Riley gang like you did, but I'd breathe a whole lot freer if it weren't pointed at me."

"Oh. Sorry." I holstered the revolver, not sure why I felt as if I needed to apologize to her.

She gathered up her knitting and stuffed it into a straw sack at the side of the chair. "You're in early. I expected you to be out for a spell."

"I should have sent a telegram?"

"Lot of good that would do, seeing as they haven't yet strung wires this far north." She squinted at me disapprovingly. "Pouting doesn't become you, Mr. Ragland."

"You've broken into my room without a warrant. Or have you got one of those in your knitting bag?"

"Guilty as charged. If you wish to register a complaint, you'll have to do so at the territorial capital." She knew that I had no intention of riding down to Yankton to file a complaint.

"I hope you have a good reason for being here, Marshal."

"Bill Riley good enough?"

My anger fizzled. "You found the thief?"

She laughed. "My, how quickly your attitude can change. No, that would be too easy. But I've been inquiring, and I have a lead for you."

"I thought this was your town? I got the feeling you wanted me to butt out."

"I do. That's why I'm telling you this." Her eyes fluttered in a particularly unsettling manner. "It seems neither the thieves nor your bounty head are in Bend City. And since I have no interest in following a couple of outlaws into the badlands, I'm passing the information on to you so's you can go do what you do best. I like my comforts, you see. A warm house. A warm bed." Her view shifted disturbingly toward my bed.

"How did—" I started to say, but my voice had suddenly pitched too high. I cleared my throat. "How did you learn this?"

"An Indian came 'round the office begging whiskey money. He said he had information on Bill Riley he was wanting to sell. I told him I wasn't buying, but he was welcome to spend a night in jail if he didn't tell me what he knew. He saw the benefit in talking."

"Was he wearing a red shirt?"

She gave me a blank look.

"Never mind." I had Chief on the brain again.

"Don't recall the color. Dirty comes close enough." Her view narrowed down some. "He looked and smelled a lot like you did when you first come to see me."

I grimaced, recalling the stench of vomit that morning.

She grabbed the grips of her knitting bag and stood. "He told me that two strangers arrived on the riverboat today. They met up with a man in the alley by the livery. He gave them a sack in exchange for an envelope. My guess is the envelope contained money. The men left by way of a buggy heading west. Nothing much west of here but badlands all the way to the Black Hills." She looked me up and down with something like longing in her eyes and then breathed out a sigh and said, "They've got five to six hours head start on you, Mr. Ragland."

"Who handed over the sack?"

She shook her head. "The Indian didn't know. But I wouldn't waste too much time wondering about that. Good night."

I closed the door behind her and leaned against it. It was a lame story with more holes than the old milk can I use for shooting practice.

CHAPTER 12

My thoughts went rampaging down one rabbit trail to another. After a little while, it was plain obvious I wasn't about to get any rest tonight. Stretched out on the bed in the dark, thinking over what she'd told me, I knew one thing for certain. Marshal Bethany Bulger wanted me out of town.

The thing I didn't know was . . . why?

The two men she'd told me about had to be the same two rumpled-suited gents she'd followed off the wharf and then later met with in her office. If so, they were known to Bulger; they weren't strangers to her. She'd lied. If they had come to town to collect old Bill, how had they got word he was here? Bulger had confirmed what I'd already found out earlier: Bend City didn't have a telegraph. If a rider had been sent to fetch them, why hadn't he simply delivered Bill and collected the money at the time?

An Injun told her, she'd claimed. That was convenient. How could anyone disprove it? If there was one thing Bend City wasn't lacking, it was Injuns.

At first I scoffed at her story, but then my thoughts took off down an unexpected trail. What if an Injun really had told her? Chief? He had, after all, taken a particular interest in the gents. Who better to have seen them make their alleyway transaction than Chief? But then, why had those two men been in the marshal's office? How had they been summoned here so quickly? And what was Bethany Bulger's part in all this?

I was no further ahead in solving the problem a half hour later as I made my way along a deserted Bend Avenue, past the now-closed saloon, and down River Street. Passing Hagmann's Fishworks, I slowed. The window panes were black as Mephistopheles's heart. Looking around, I casually tried the door. Locked. I continued on down to the wharf at a leisurely pace just in case someone was watching and stood there a while looking out over the black water where ribbons of moonlight meandered off slow eddies. A mist had risen from the water, and a cool, low fog had come ashore. I judged the time at maybe two o' the clock.

A little distance down the riverbank a flicker of firelight poked through the scrawny stand of cottonwood trees that had somehow escaped the logger's ax. I remembered I had intended to investigate that campsite. Tomorrow maybe. Tonight I had other plans.

In the cooler air the mosquitoes were tolerable. Even so, those more hardy individuals didn't waste any time sighting in on me. Swatting them away, I moved off toward Sawmill Road, past the corral alongside the warehouse where that sorry mule stood with its back to the river, its head down.

Before reaching Sawmill Road I turned into a narrow gap between the Murry & Murry Territorial Transfer Bank and a ship's chandler shop—the same passageway where I'd spied Chief lurking the day before.

I felt my way along in the dark, trash crunching beneath my boots. The sound of someone pounding a hammer drifted faintly down from up in town. I wondered briefly who was working this late into the night. Another passage running parallel to the river cut across the one I was following. I took it and shortly stepped out onto a blind alley that ended abruptly at the loading platform for Hagmann's Fishworks.. A flight of six steps climbed to the platform, where there were some barrels, a pile of dark crates, and a door.

The door was locked, but a window high up on the wall had been left open a little to air out the smell of fish. Rolling a barrel beneath it, I pulled myself up and inside and then hunkered there waiting for my eyes to adjust to the weak moon glow coming through the dingy panes of glass. When I got to seeing better I spied a lamp on a desk with a box of matches beside it.

Even with the wick turned low, the lamp cast too much light—at least to my sensitive eyes. A small pasteboard box from a shelf shielded it some and directed it away from the window.

I was in the fish works's business office. Sniffing the air, I didn't detect the presence of Bill Riley, but it was hard to be sure. The fishy smell worsened as I crept down the stairs into the salting works.

Brine barrels filled the main floor, as did two long tables for gutting and scaling. Along one wall stood something like an oven large enough to walk into. It turned out to be a meat smoker. Nearby hundreds of smoked fish hung by strings tied to their tails. They dangled from the ceiling like a bead curtain. A sort of fish forest, I mused.

My spirits sank. If Bill Riley was here, there'd be no way to discover him by his smell. The place had already begun to close my sinuses. Bending low, I crept beneath the dangling fish, the stink making my head spin. Nothing interesting was on the other side of them. Only the back wall of the building.

Back out in the main room I began opening cabinets and pulling out drawers in a methodical manner, investigating each while trying to keep my pasteboard shield turned to reflect light away from the windows. Mostly what I discovered were bags of salt, fillet knives, sharpening wheels and stones, burlap bags of wood chips for the smoker, rags, towels, aprons . . .

The door gave a metallic rattle. I froze, listening. Someone on the sidewalk outside had pushed a key into the lock. I blew out the lamp and backed into the dangling forest of fish.

The door opened, and two or three people came in. I couldn't tell for sure how many until one of them lit a lamp. Not surprisingly, Henry Hagmann's face appeared in the glow. What did surprise me were the other two people with him. Wally Mace and Bethany Bulger.

Mace had his hands pushed deep into his trouser pockets and kept looking over his shoulder at the door as if expecting someone else.

"Let's see it again." Bethany's voice sounded tired, and her face showed it.

Hagmann led them to a cabinet on the wall that looked to have been built like a safe. Iron straps crisscrossed the door, and a big padlock stood guard over it. He passed the lamp to Mace, drew a ring of keys from his pocket, and began flipping through them. Finding the right one, he turned to the lock.

Tucked away like I was among the forest of smoked fish, I heard the lock snap open. The door hinges creaked, and the three of them gathered closer, Mace lifting the lamp higher.

The cabinet door blocked my view of what was inside. I eased into another spot, trying not to disturb the scaly drapery hanging about my head, but I was still unable to see.

"Uncover it, and let's have a look," Marshal Bulger said.

I weighed my chance of sneaking in a little closer unseen but decided against it until I was sure they had Bill Riley's head.

"Hmm," Mace intoned. "Looks to be all there."

" 'Course it's all there," Hagmann growled. "You think I'd cheat you?"

"Settle down, Henry. I didn't mean anything by that."

"You two back off each other," Bulger said. "I swear, you're a fine pair. A cat and dog long as I've known you. Don't understand how Brian put up with you long as he did." She exhaled an exasperated breath and stepped between them.

"Can't even conduct a little business on the side without one or the other of you getting your hackles up."

Hagmann said, "You want to take it now, Beth?"

"No!" The notion seemed to have appalled her. "First I want to see the color of their money, but they won't show me that until they see a sample, proving we still have it."

I got a little nervous. *Sample?* What were they going to do—cut off an ear or something?

Mace said, "Sure. Just so long as you don't give them anything until it's time to make the exchange." He looked at Hagmann. "Remove a piece for Beth to show them."

Hagmann took something from a nearby fish-cleaning table—I couldn't see what from where I stood hidden amongst the smoked fish. He turned back to the cabinet and a moment later passed a small cloth-wrapped item to Bulger.

She said, "I never wanted to get involved in this from the start. But since I am"—she stuck the cloth into her handbag—"I want this deal to go down without a hitch. Only one bump in the road as I see it."

Hagmann said, "That Ragland fellow."

"He's suspicious and smart. He's not going to give up until he finds Riley or turns this town upside down looking. That might be a problem for us if he catches wind of our little deal here." Her view shifted between the two men. "I've planted a thought in Ragland's head, and if I'm right, he's making his way west by now, or will be, come morning."

Hagmann said, "That might win us some time, but he's a tracker. It won't be long before he figures out you sent him on a fool's errand. When he does, he'll be back pronto." Hagmann glanced at Mace. "Where are the buyers now?"

Mace gave a resolute shake of his head. "Not at my place. I don't want any fingers pointing back to me should this deal blow up. I've got big plans, and cooling my heels behind bars ain't going to get them done."

I hadn't considered the criminality of stealing a dead man, or at least a part of a dead man, but I wouldn't put it past some slick lawyer to scrounge up a couple laws against it.

"Nobody is going to be cooling their heels, Wally. Not so long as I'm the law hereabouts." Her words had taken on a confident tone. It seemed to fit her well. I was finding it harder and harder not to like the woman—even if she was a thief and a liar.

"That's only until the territorial marshal down in Yankton gets around to straightening things out up here," Mace said dourly.

"He's had nearly eight months to do so. If he was going to *straighten things out,* he'd have done it by now."

"So, where *are* they?" Hagmann pressed, impatient.

She drew a breath. "Didn't want them mingling. Their accent was bound to draw attention, and attention is the last thing we want. I put them up in Harel's old place. Being that it's at the edge of town, I'm counting on no one noticing if stray light gets past the curtains."

Hagmann laughed. "And if anyone does notice, they'll think it's another one of those ancient Indian ghosts."

Wally Mace chuckled. "Superstitions are useful tools."

Bethany Bulger didn't seem to find humor in that. "I'm to meet with them first thing in the morning." She inclined her head at the cabinet. "Keep near that, Henry. Once the deal is done, we need to move quickly. I want them gone before Ragland comes back and starts poking around again."

"That might be a problem," Mace noted. "No telling when the next riverboat will show up."

Bethany Bulger said, "They plan on getting a trap from the livery and driving to the railhead at Sioux City. Lock it up, Henry. Let's call it a night, gentlemen."

"What's left of it," Mace said sounding dour again.

Hagmann locked the cabinet and blew out the lamp.

Soon as the door closed behind them I scooted from the forest of dangling fish and began examining the cabinet. I dared not light the lamp again even if I could. I'd left the matches upstairs. The weak light from the window showed a cabinet stoutly constructed, obviously with the idea in mind to make it safe to store valuables—cash most likely. I ran a hand across the iron straps bolted along the edges and crisscrossing the thick wooden sides and door. The iron was stout, a quarter inch or more.

I gave the heavy lock a tug just in case it hadn't latched. It had. There was a little movement in the door. The iron hasp had a small amount of play in it, enough to allow for a gap wide enough to slip a knife blade in . . . or a crowbar.

The fish-cleaning table nearby held a variety of sharp items—stout boning knives, thin fillet knives, long-nosed pliers for removing hooks, and various toothed implements for scaling, but no crowbar. I stumbled about in the dark for a while bumping into tables and barrels, finding nothing strong enough to burst the cabinet open.

I needed to find a tool to pry with, and I was running out of night.

Retracing my steps up the stairs, I returned the lamp to the desktop and climbed out through the window, lowering myself onto the barrel. The air was cooler with an odd, yet somehow familiar, stench hanging about.

The stench wasn't exactly like fish—more like stale piss. I didn't think too much about it as I started down the alleyway.

Coming out on a little street that ran north to south, the sound of hammering again reached me.

Who would be doing carpentry work at this hour?

CHAPTER 13

Somewhere off in the distance came the steady rasp of a handsaw attacking a piece of wood. The sound grew louder as I followed it into an alleyway, right up to the back door of the Buffalo Wallow Saloon. A light showed against the single, dingy windowpane in the door.

I peeked inside.

Bobby Parker was busy exercising his arm against a stout board. By the looks of the small stack of slim boards on the floor and the growing pile of sawdust beneath the sawhorses, he'd been at it quite a while. I remembered the box Parker had been building.

He happened to look up just then and gave a start at seeing my nose against the windowpane. I don't think he recognized me at first, and then his startled look turned to puzzlement . . . or maybe it was worry. He set the saw aside and, brushing himself off, opened the door for me.

"Mr. Ragland?" he said wiping sweat from around his puffy eyes with the corner of a dirty, green bandanna about his neck. There was a note of uncertainty in his voice, or was it caution? I couldn't blame him.

I said, "Heard all this hammering and sawing and said to myself, who'd be so almighty industrious in the middle of the night?"

Still cautious, he said, "I might ask the same of you. It's well past the witching hour."

"Couldn't sleep." I grinned. "Amazing how fresh air will cure insomnia."

"Ahem." His eyes narrowed to a scowl.

"I see you don't believe me."

"I'd easier believe that you're out prowling about looking for Mr. Bill Riley's head."

"You are an astute fellow, Mr. Parker."

"Any luck?" He asked to be polite, but his impatient tone made it clear he wished me to be gone.

"I have my nose to a trail," I said in a vague manner.

"Well, I wish you luck. Good night, Mr. Ragland." He started to close the door.

I stuck a boot in the gap. "I was wondering if you might be able to help me."

Now he did look worried. "How?" he asked, taking a dry swallow.

"I need to borrow a tool. A crowbar, to be exact."

He looked surprised, and then suspicious. "What *exactly* is it you are up to?"

"Can't *exactly* say at the moment, but I'll bring the crowbar back soon as I'm done using it. Promise."

"Can't or won't?" Parker pressed.

"Sort of the same things, aren't they?" I smiled.

He stared at me a long moment before finally pulling the door open. "I hope I don't regret this." He went to a dark corner, coming back with an iron bar. It was heavy and strong, just what I needed.

"You won't," I promised, casting a glance at the project in the middle of the storeroom floor. He appeared to be building a shallow box, with the corners mitered and fitted with care. "If you don't mind my curiosity, what are you building?"

"A trophy case to hang on the wall." He sounded annoyed and plainly wanted me to leave.

108

"Trophies?"

"Base Ball. We're going to put together our own league. *The Bend City Injuns.*" He stepped back, hefted a make-believe bat over his shoulder and hit a make-believe ball out the connecting door into the dark saloon. "I come from Chicago, you know. The Chicago White Stockings play there. Marvelous game. Ever gone to one?"

"Never seen a real game, but I hear it's getting to be a right popular pastime."

"The National Association of Base Ball Players has over five hundred leagues and growing every month." He escorted me to the back door. "Good night, Mr. Ragland."

I took the hint this time and saluted him with the crowbar. "I'll just leave this outside against the wall when I'm through with it."

He nodded and closed the door behind me. The iron bolt made a solid clank as Parker slid it into place.

His behavior had been strange, but then, my prowling about at three in the morning couldn't exactly be called normal. I hurried back to Hagmann's Fishworks and hauled myself up through the open window. I knew my way this time and left the lamp on the desk, feeling my way down the stairs with a grip on the handrail, creeping cautiously past the gutting tables to the cabinet.

Wedging the bar into the gap, I worked at the strong box a while. Whoever had built it had done a masterful job. The hinges strained, and the wood groaned, but the iron straps held, and the lock stood like a bank vault door against my attack.

I kept at it, stopping now and again at the small sounds coming from the dark. Rats, likely. This place was sure to be a rodent magnet. The stench seemed to get worse, if that was possible.

Having no luck on the door itself, I spent some effort prying at the hasp. When that didn't work, I tried to spring the lock by levering it back and forth. After a while I stopped and just stared at the cabinet. I needed to be smarter than the lock. "You think you've bested me, do you," I told it. "Well, we'll see about that."

"Talking to oneself is a sign of insanity," a voice said from somewhere nearby.

I lurched around, shoulders hunched, my view darting about the blackness. Instinctively my hand found the butt of my revolver.

The voice said, "There are easier ways to break into a locked box, you know."

"Where are you," I demanded, a sharp fingernail running up my spine.

"No, not over there. Over here."

My view followed the voice to an indistinct shadow sitting on top of one of the gutting tables, a pair of knees drawn up, hugged by a pair of arms. "Who are you?"

He gave a short laugh, unfolded himself, and swung his feet to the floor. "Fortunately for you, no kinsman of Bill Riley, or you'd be playing a harp by now."

I recognized the voice then . . . and the smell. "Chief?"

"You don't let a man get much rest, do you, Mr. Ragland," he said in perfect English, without a hint of being impaired with whiskey.

My hand still gripped the butt of the Remington as he moved. "What do you mean?"

He came closer and stopped. "I mean, you scurry about in the night like a fox rooting out rats." He was near enough now for me to see him clearly, and for the stink to lighten my brain. He took something from his vest pocket that made a faint click and turned it toward the window. "Three thirty. By now most men are asleep, except for you and Mr. Parker."

"I'm hunting something," I said, off balance by his presence and his unexpectedly sober demeanor.

"Yes, I know." The watch cover clicked shut and went back into the vest pocket. "Bill Riley."

"What happened to your Injun talk?"

"Cambridge." He looked at the crowbar in my hand, and then at the cabinet. "You think Bill Riley is in there?"

I was still rattled, I'll admit, and trying to make some sense out of him being here. He'd plainly been following me, and not just to beg whiskey money. I didn't know what to do with the Injun, but so far he hadn't made a threatening move, so I held off shooting him. "It's the only place in Bend City left. I've turned this miserable town inside out."

"I know." A faint smile moved across his face. "I don't think you'll find what you're looking for in there."

His confidence irritated me. "What do you know about it? And, by the way, why have you been following me?"

He shrugged. "You were a stranger in town. And you bore a most intriguing odor."

"Well, I can attest to the fact that you're an authority on odors. What is that smell you tote around? Dog piss?"

"Badger. I find it preferable to that of rotting human flesh."

I ignored the jab. "Do you tail every stranger who comes to town?"

"Pretty much. Until I figure out who they are and what they are up to." His speech was a little stilted, like he'd learned his English from someone obsessed with things like proper diction.

He inclined his head at the cabinet. "I will wager that you won't find Bill Riley in there."

I hadn't figured Chief out, so I played along, hoping he'd tip his hand. "What do you want to bet? I got fifty cents that says he is. That'll buy you a whole bottle of Parker's whiskey."

He shuddered visibly and shook his head. "I would rather not. We Aboriginal Americans don't handle our whiskey very well . . . even cut three to one with river water. I have a better idea. If Riley is in there, I will go on my way and not bother you again. If, however, Mr. Riley is not in there, you help me finish my job, and I'll help you find old Bill."

"Your job? Other than the handful of Cheyenne Hagmann's got fishing for him, I didn't get the impression Injuns around here did much of anything except beg whiskey."

"Have we an agreement?"

I stuck out a hand, and we shook on it. "Deal. What is your job . . . exactly?"

"First let's see what's behind that door."

I turned back at the cabinet. "Good luck. It's built like a St. Louis bank vault. I've been working at it for most half an hour and so far only managed to make a mess of the wood." I wedged the crowbar into the gap again.

"There's your problem," Chief said. "You are using seventeenth-century technology to solve a nineteenth-century problem." His tone held an arrogant edge.

I scowled at him. "If you've got a better idea, let's hear it."

Chief dipped into the possibles bag he carried over his shoulder, removed something that looked like a bunch of metal playing cards, and began unfolding them. They all cleverly snapped together to make a brass box, small enough to hold in his palm. A match flared, and the wick inside the box sputtered to life. He closed the final panel that must have been fitted with a lens of some sort, because the light that came through it focused in a narrow beam upon the lock.

"That is a Post and Company railroad switch lock. Very high quality."

I said, "I couldn't break it open."

"They are designed that way to prevent someone from throwing a switch and sending a train down the wrong tracks." He spoke with a certain authority, as if railroad locks were a thing he knew intimately. "Here, hold this." He passed me the lamp and fished a small pouch from his possibles bag, unrolling it. The pouch contained maybe a half-dozen slim, steel picks. Selecting two of them, he thumbed back the lock's cover plate and inserted them into the keyhole. Holding pressure on one, he wiggled the other with a surgeon's gentle touch. The lock snapped open.

"Where'd you learn to do that?"

Chief looked over with a smug grin that also annoyed me. Maybe I was irked at myself because I suddenly felt very foolish.

I said, "Think you're pretty clever, don't you."

"Spending half an hour with a crowbar with nothing to show for it is your idea of clever?" He slipped the lock off the hasp, and I shined the lantern inside. Flashes of red, green, amber, and deep sapphire blue glinted in its beam. My jaw went slack at the sight of rubies and emeralds, and the unmistakable color of gold, all of it sitting in a nest of rich red velvet. "What is it?"

"That is the coronation crown of the kingdom of Mirratavia. Or, to be more precise, the crown that Crown Prince Frederick von Lipsig was supposed to wear on the day he became king."

"*Mirratavia?* Never heard of the place." Something scratched at the back of my brain.

Next to the crown was a small pile of jewels and gold chains, and a dagger in a golden sheath encrusted with emeralds. "What's all this doing here?"

"The very question that Lloyd's would like to have an answer to, and one that we are going to find out."

"We?"

He raised his eyebrows. "You forgot our wager so soon?"

"No, course not," I said, averting my eyes before they gave away the lie.

Chief closed the cabinet door and snapped the lock back in place.

"You leaving the stuff?" For some reason I'd got the impression that this was what he'd been after all along.

"I could have taken it any time I wanted to these last few weeks. It's safer locked up here than at my campsite."

"You knew it was here all along?"

"We need to talk, Mr. Ragland."

Well, so much for impressions.

Chapter 14

With dawn but an hour off, Chief and I sat near his campfire in a grove of cottonwood trees down near the water's edge. The fire had been only a dying bed of coals when we'd arrived after leaving the fish works by way of the saloon's back door, where I left Bobby Parker's crowbar as promised. The saloon had been dark and Parker gone—to bed, I assumed, but that was only a guess.

I slapped and fidgeted while Chief steadied a coffee pot on a small bed of coals he'd dragged off to one side of the stone fire ring with a stick. The mosquitoes were still on the prowl, but the cool night air had worn them out considerably. For some reason, Chief seemed unaffected by the insects.

I said, "They don't like the taste of Injun blood?"

He reached around inside a sack by his bedroll and came up with a small lard tin. "Try some of this?"

I took it. "What is it?"

Feigning an accent, he said, "Old *Injun* recipe. Mosquitoes no like."

I unscrewed the lid, took a cautious whiff. The stench nearly knocked me over. "This smells like you. What's in it?"

"Fever grass, horseradish, fermented armadillo liver, and badger piss. Mosquitoes hate it. So do most other critters. Even water moccasins. But not bees. Something about it attracts bees. Not a large problem so long as you don't get one under your shirt."

I pushed the tin back at him. "I'd rather have the mosquitoes, thank you."

"Mosquitoes carry disease and parasites."

"What disease?"

"Malaria, deer fever, dengue fever."

"Dengue fever?" I scowled. "This is the Dakota Territory, not Panama.

He shrugged and put the tin back into the sack. "You want to take that chance, okay with me. I'm not your mother. Being stupid isn't a crime in a free country . . . yet."

I ignored him. "You got a name, or will Chief do?"

"Robert LaCroix. But Chief will work."

"French? I didn't think the French had many dealings with the Cheyenne or Sioux."

"I wouldn't know. My father was a Creek planter. He had a plantation in Georgia. I was a b—an accident."

"Oh. Sorry."

"Nothing to be sorry about. My mother was the daughter of a neighboring plantation. She was white, and between the two of them I learned a lot about both cultures. My father was wealthy and honored his . . . responsibilities. He saw to it that I received an education, and when I was old enough, he sent me off to England. That was shortly before the War for Southern Independence." He looked at me. "Sure you don't want to try some of it?"

"I'm sure." I slapped a hungry one that left a big spot of blood on my palm. "I've been thinking about those jewels. I recall now a newspaper story I read while soaking in the barbershop bathtub. It happened in Omaha, right?"

Chief—LaCroix—nodded.

I said, "That robbery was months ago."

"Almost a year ago. Frederick and his entourage changed trains in Omaha on their cross-country tour to hunt buffalo.

They were bound for Sacramento, where the jewels were to be put on display. Afterwards, they were to board a steamer for Russia—another showing scheduled for St. Petersburg—and then several more appointments with European monarchies as Frederick and his party traveled by rail back to Mirratavia."

"What's the point? I mean, other than for him to show off his wealth and shoot buffalo along the way?"

"Wealth?" Chief laughed and tossed a branch into the flames. "That might actually have been the point. You see, Mirratavia is a tiny kingdom shouldered between Switzerland and Germany— part of the old Prussian empire. An ink drop on the map. It's nestled down a little valley near a couple of postage-stamp–size ex-Prussian duchies. What wealth they actually have might be better measured in scenery than in gold. That crown and the small pile of jewelry with it probably accounts for a quarter of the kingdom's net worth."

I frowned. "Sounds like this Frederick fellow was trying to build a reputation for himself. Maybe he figured if he showed off some fancy-looking gewgaws, the other kingdoms might take him and this Mirratavia place seriously. Seems a pretty risky enterprise if what you say is true."

"Or a very clever gambit."

I slapped the back of my neck and sent another mosquito on to its eternal reward. "How so?"

"Insurance fraud can be very profitable."

I saw where he was going. "Especially if it can double your net worth. You're a detective?"

"Pinkerton." Chief retrieved two tin cups from his bag and tapped them on a rock to evict any critters that had taken up residence in them.

"Pinkerton's? Why would they send an Injun to do a job like this?"

He looked amused. "It's not like I'd stand out in a crowd in a place like Bend City."

"True enough. Injuns are mighty thick in these parts, and, to a white man, one Injun looks like another." I added that last part as a jab, but he didn't seem to notice. "Let me see if I got this straight. Prince Frederick arranged to have his own treasure stolen and then went home and made a claim against the insurance. The company settles up with him. He gets the money and then sends his representatives—those two men in the rumpled suits this morning—back to fetch the items."

"More or less. You are missing a couple of pieces of the puzzle. The crown and jewelry were insured for four million mirramarks."

I whistled. "Four million."

"Mirramarks," Chief emphasized.

"How much is that in dollars?"

His head tilted as he ciphered it out in his brain. "About two hundred thousand dollars, give or take."

I whistled. "Two hundred grand."

"The other piece you're missing is that the jewels aren't worth more than maybe two million mirramarks tops. I have an appraisal from the jeweler who examined the pieces when they first went on display in New York City."

My dealings with insurance companies were slim to none, but my future father-in-law did occasionally truck with them through his business ventures. I said, "You'd think insurance companies would be more careful. Who'd be dumb enough to insure that stuff for twice its value?"

"Lloyd's."

"Who?"

"Lloyd's of London. They'll insure almost anything so long as you agree to their terms. They're not an insurance company in the usual sense, more like a consortium of wealthy business owners who come together to spread the risks around among their members. Lloyd's calls their members *Names.*"

I gave Chief a skeptical look. "How can they stay in business doing that?"

A patient smile moved across his greasy face. "They don't literally call them names, Mr. Ragland. *Names,* collectively, is how Lloyd's refers to their members."

His patronizing tone rankled. I'd thought Chief annoying back in the fishworks. Now I was certain of it. Chief had an annoying talent of being most agreeable while making you feel knee high to a frog.

"Okay. So, the *kingdom of Mirratavia* is a member *Name* of Lloyd's?" I smashed a blood-sucking skeeter that'd managed to get through my shirtsleeve.

Chief shook his head. "That would be too easy, wouldn't it?"

I rolled my eyes. "If you were a skeeter, I'd swat you."

He grinned. "This is where it gets interesting. A few years ago, the kingdom of Mirratavia purchased a foundering corporation for pennies on the dollar. Blackpool Cargoes. At one time Blackpool was a big player in the slave trade. Lloyd's generated much of its income from the late seventeenth century until the early years of this one insuring slave ships. After England outlawed the slave trade, many companies went out of business and fell off Lloyd's Names list. Blackpool Cargoes managed to struggle along, engaged mainly in the spice trade to the West Indies. But the Fates were not kind to Blackpool. It lost ships and customers, and in the end was just a shell with few assets. One asset, however, was quite valuable. The corporation was still listed as a Lloyd's Name."

I said, "This is beginning to look like a swindle that's been a long time in the planning."

"It appears to have been carefully planned with the intent of enriching a failing state. Over there in Europe, especially with Prussia declining and the German empire rising, if you can't defend your castle, your neighbor takes it away from you."

"And a few million mirramarks will buy a lot of Enfield rifles and Armstrong artillery pieces." An image came to my head of two castles standing shoulder to shoulder pummeling each other with cannon perched upon their parapets.

"That's what Lloyd's thinks."

"Did they pay up?" I asked, whacking a mosquito off my cheek. Chief offered his magic salve again, and I almost gave in, then shook my head and waved it away.

"They did settle the claim, and then they contacted their agent in the States, who hired Pinkerton's to find the proof of fraud they need to go after Mirratavia."

"Can an insurance company go after an entire country?"

"There are legal and not so legal ways of doing it. A monarchy isn't like a republic. In general, kings and such are an inbred bunch. It's practically one big extended family over there. Most are related through birth or marriage and more often than not are at each other's throats. European wars are mainly family squabbles. It wouldn't take much effort for Lloyd's to convince a few wealthy Names to put financial pressure on an insignificant kingdom the size of Mirratavia. If that didn't work—well, there are plenty of second and third cousins perched on postage-stamp duchies who'd love to expand their little plot of land, especially if Lloyd's is willing to foot the bill for the war."

Chief gave me some time to digest all that. I had never thought much about royalty and kingdoms and insurance fraud. None of those things had been of concern to me and how I lived my life. And they still weren't. My concern was locating Bill Riley's head, turning it over to the paymaster at Fort Leavenworth, collecting three thousand dollars in bounty money, and then hurrying on to St. Louis to confront Pierre Toutant and ask for Francine's hand in marriage.

But here I was, hunched over a campfire on the dark bank of

the Big Muddy—Missouri River, USA—swatting mosquitoes, taking a cup of coffee from a Pinkerton detective Injun with a bigger vocabulary than Mr. Webster, and with more world-traveled miles under his moccasins than I could ever hope to have.

The morning sky had grown gray and pink to the east. I peered at Chief over the rim of my coffee cup. He looked arrogantly confident and smugly patient, graciously giving me as much time as I needed to think over what I'd just learned. And the whole time he didn't once swat a bloody mosquito! It was as unlikely a situation as I'd ever imagined myself in, and even after Chief's neat explanation of the escapades of one Prince/King Frederick, I had more questions than answers.

"What does Marshal Bulger have to do with all this?" I asked.

"Actually it was her late husband who got her involved. Brian Bulger worked for the Union Pacific Railroad in Omaha when this scheme was concocted. After the deed was done, Brian was fortuitously appointed deputy territorial marshal. He'd put in for the job months earlier. He was assigned to Bend City but died unexpectedly—horse threw him and broke his neck. Bethany took over the job. The law being what it is out here—or should I say what it *isn't*—the territorial marshal in charge of the Dakota Territory hasn't seen the need to appoint a successor to Brian.

"Being a marshal, no one would be suspicious of him and start nosing around Bend City. Brian, Henry Hagmann, Walter Mace, and Harel Lemuel were all in on the theft."

"Harel Lemuel? Weren't him and his wife run out of town by a ghost? Something about dead Injuns stalking their bedroom at midnight?"

"Blame it on us Indians." Chief laughed. "There's no truth to the story, but it's something folks around here truly believe."

I double-slapped a pair of bloodsuckers working my neck. "It did kinda sound farfetched to me when I heard it."

Chief offered his tin of mosquito salve again. After hunkering there around the campfire with him for a while now, my nose had become used to the stink. Hesitating, I took it.

He said, "It took longer to settle up the insurance claim than they'd counted on. As the months passed, they all knew it was only a matter of time before their role in Frederick's scheme was found out. Harel got cold feet. Since ghost stories are popular here in Bend City, he and Alice left town on some silly excuse about Indian ghosts haunting their house, which conveniently just happens to be over by the cemetery. They claimed that Mace generously purchased their place. That was a cover story. What Mace really bought was their share of the reward. I suspect he paid something quite a bit less than what Harel and Alice would have received had they waited for the Mirratavia agents to arrive with the payoff. Mace keeps a tight fist on his money."

"So I've discovered." I opened the tin and cautiously smelled the salve, still not convinced I wanted any part of it. "I overheard them say they were going to do the deal tomorrow."

"I suspected so. We need to be there when they do. I want to catch King Frederick's agents making the payoff. You being along will be the witness I need to make this ironclad."

Chief made it sound so simple that my skin crawled. "There's only one big problem," I said, gratified to note his smug smile falter some. "The way I see it, the law hereabouts is on the king's side, and I'd be mighty surprised if those two agents of his aren't well armed and trained to protect themselves and all those jewels. Just how do you plan to catch them?"

He thought a moment, that irritating smile moving slowly back in place. A glint of mischief flashed in his dark eyes. "I was going to let you handle that part."

"Were you, now?"

"I hear T. J. Ragland is the fastest gun hand this side of the Missouri River. A man without a single fearful bone in his entire body. In a blaze of gun fire, he single-handedly drew down on all ten of the fearsome Riley gang desperadoes, and when the gun smoke cleared and they were all shot full of holes, he skinned their hides and hung them out on a tree to dry."

"Ha-ha, funny. You forgot the part about me bushwhacking them first."

"I was saving that for later."

I caught an hour or two of sleep and awoke with the sun well above the horizon and pushing long morning shadows across the ground. The air was warming, and the mosquitoes had all gone home for the day. Chief was still sawing logs. I stood, stretched, and stoked up the fire. The coffee pot had a little left in it, so I set it back on the coals and then wandered off to take care of business. When I returned, Chief was awake, sitting cross-legged on his blanket, staring at nothing in particular.

"Morning already?" he mumbled, sounding thoroughly appalled.

"There's still some coffee in the pot."

"Ugh." Chief looked up at me. "It was already two days old last night."

"Tasted two days old . . . last night, but I was too polite to mention it. We can go to the Big Muddy Café."

Chief shook his head. "Eating a civilized breakfast in a civilized café will ruin my cover, not to mention your reputation. It's better we are not seen together."

I didn't raise any objection to that suggestion.

Chapter 15

Maybe Chief didn't want to eat in a "civilized café," but I had no such misgivings. I trudged up the hill into town and through the Big Muddy's front door. The place had a few more customers than usual, and I was pleased to see it, knowing how Margaret and Franklin Collins were struggling to pull both ends of a financial rope together.

Some folks looked up as I entered, and I could see noses begin to wrinkle. Well, I couldn't fault them, but then they hadn't spent the night down by the river where mosquitoes hunted in packs. Chief's salve surely worked at warding off mosquitoes . . . and most humans, too.

I took a table. Mrs. Collins came over to take my order, her mouth set, stern lines deepening about her eyes. "What'll you have this morning?" she said sharply. I smelled bad, but I hadn't expected the salve to have such an effect on her.

"Just some eggs, over easy, a slice of ham and coffee," I said, wondering what had happened. She turned to leave. "Where's Franklin?" I asked.

Her barbed-wire view came back around. "Out."

The way she'd said it, I figured our conversation was at an end, but there was more on Margaret Collins's mind. "If you must know, he's got another damn fool notion in his head. He's going off to 'make us both rich.' But he won't. He never does. This time he'll end up dead, and I'll be a widow." She made it sound as if she considered this to be somehow all my fault.

I wasn't about to ask what sort of notion could cause such dire destruction. I didn't want to stoke the fire any higher, as it was hot enough already. Taking the coward's way, I asked instead, "Can you talk him out of it?" I seemed unable to take my eyes off of hers. Past the worry I saw in them a deep, liquid fear. I was concerned and defensive at the same time, and I wanted to hug her like I would a frightened child.

She deflated like a balloon with a slow leak. "When Franklin gets a notion in his head, changing it is like trying to shake a coon from a tree." She looked around, indicating the café with a sweep of her arm. "This place stuck out in the middle of nowhere was one of his get-rich ideas. I hate Bend City. Hate this land with its biting black flies, awful mosquitoes, and choking pollen that near suffocates me during the spring bloom."

She was struggling now to hold back tears. Although she'd kept her voice low, she was drawing attention to herself. I felt eyes on me, too, as if somehow I was the source of her troubles.

"Why don't you leave?"

The deflation was complete. She stood there a defeated woman. "I have threatened him with that . . . but I won't leave Franklin. I love my husband. We took vows. For better or worse." She drew herself up, calling upon some inner strength, turned, and hurried back through the door to the kitchen.

I respected Margaret Collins. She was a strong woman who'd stick by her man even when he was wrong, even when his decisions made life a misery. That was how it ought to be. That's how it would be between Francine and me once we were married. I took comfort in that thought until a little cloud of uncertainty drifted overhead and perched in front of the sunny glow that had been Francine's smile. Something like a steel band tightened around my chest.

I shifted my view out the window to where Chief sat alongside the saloon, not begging, just scrunched down on the bench there, arms folded across his chest, chin down as if napping. But he wasn't napping. He was as alert as an eagle, keeping track of everything going on around him. Admittedly, there wasn't much to keep track of yet, as the morning was still young, but we both knew that would change.

After breakfast I made my way toward the abandoned Lemuel residence to keep a watch for the two Mirratavia agents. According to the plan Chief and I had sketched out around the campfire swatting mosquitoes—well, one of us was swatting—Chief would keep watch over the fish works and saloon while I kept an eye on the house near the cemetery.

The door to the marshal's office was open when I passed by it. A glance showed me that no one was in the building. I strolled on, keeping an eye out for Marshal Bulger and the two foreigners.

At the corner of Bend and Sawmill I stopped and let my view travel slowly up toward the cemetery, looking for signs of those agents out stretching their legs, or peeking from behind the curtains hanging in one of the two windows of Harel and Alice Lemuel's abandoned house. The marshal had said they were camping out there. Well, if they were there, they were keeping their heads down. King Frederick wouldn't have sent amateurs on an important job like this. Most likely they were soldiers, or whatever European kingdoms called 'em these days. I was pretty sure the employment of knights in shiny armor with swords and lances had passed into history long ago.

I scanned the roadway up to the fence that hugged the town's sad little graveyard. A figure stood beyond it. Bethany Bulger was alone, her head bent toward Brian's gravestone. The slight morning breeze brushed the hem of her dress. Although I didn't much care for the woman, I did admire how she'd taken over Brian's job; she was doing a pretty good job at it, even if she was mixed up in this Mirratavia affair.

She didn't move for a long time, and then her shoulders gave a little jerk and she stood straighter and started for the gate where that old cottonwood tree stood. I spun on my heels, not wanting to be seen. I was supposed to be running down make-believe thieves in some very real and desolate badlands. I made it to Toby McGill's livery stable and stood back in the shadows of the big doors watching Bethany coming down Sawmill Road. She turned left onto Bend Avenue. The intervening buildings blocked my view. I was pretty sure she was either headed back to her office, or to Hagmann's Fishworks. If the latter, Chief would be on her tail.

"I was just going to go looking for you," Toby McGill said from somewhere deep inside his big barn.

I turned and spied him sauntering in from the back corrals carrying a bucket with the handles of a couple curry combs and a big hoof trimmer sticking out. He hung the bucket on a hook and came across the dusty floor, moving like a man with a sore back.

"About an hour ago two fellows come in here looking for a berline and a horse."

"A berline?"

He grinned. "That's what they called it. They hunted some for the right word, but I knew what they was asking for. They had a funny accent so I figured berline is what they called a buggy over wherever they come from. When I showed them what I had, they powwowed in words I didn't know, and one of them pulled out a pouch of money."

"They rented a buggy?"

He sniffed the air looking around, his nose taking a wrinkle. "Nope. They *bought* a buggy, and a horse, too—a pretty good mare. They paid with a handful of gold coins the likes of which I'd never seen before, but the metal was yellow and weighed about right. See?" McGill fished one of the coins from his pocket. It was a little smaller than a twenty-dollar piece, stamped with a castle on one side and a bearded face wearing a crown on the other. Fancy leaf-like work encircled the stampings, and around the edge were some words in a language I didn't recognize.

McGill said, "After they pulled out of here I got to thinking that those two might have something to do with your problem. I know they only arrived in town yesterday, and it's not likely they're involved in stealing Bill Riley's head, but I was gonna tell you, like I promised I would." He sniffed again. "Is that stink coming from you?" he asked.

"It keeps mosquitoes at bay."

"Smells Injun-like."

"Indeed it does. Which way did they head?"

"South."

"If I recall my geography, there's not a whole lot south of here except Nebraska. Did they say where?"

He stepped back a long pace. "They weren't awful chatty, but at one point they unfolded one of those UP tourist maps and studied it some. You know the kind what's filled with little pictures of all the sights along the rail line from Omaha to San Francisco Bay?"

"I've seen one once," I said, distracted. Those agents leaving town so soon hadn't been in our plans. We'd figured they'd make the swap at the fish works, or the marshal's office, and that we'd catch them in the act.

McGill was yammering on about the stink of my mosquito repellent. I said, "Think I'll take Blue Shanks for a spell to give her some exercise."

He grinned, knowing what I had in mind.

I said in the way of a defense, "The way you're fancying up to her with your oats and curry combs, she's liable to get fat and lazy."

"Sure, Mr. Ragland," McGill said, playing along.

"I wouldn't want her to get the idea this easy living was a permanent arrangement."

"Stretching her legs is a dandy idea. She'll fancy a good trot after all the coddling I've given her. I recommend the south road. Lots of pretty scenery down along the river. I'll go fetch her for you."

Judging by the way he hurried off, I suspect he was anxious to put distance between himself and Chief's mosquito remedy.

Blue Shanks moved grudgingly beneath me. She'd become used to easy living under McGill's care, and it would take a mile or two to work the stubbornness out of her. I gave her a taste of my spurs, and that got her attention. She quickened her gait a mite.

We turned the corner onto Bend Avenue. I spied Chief up ahead, now leaning against the corner of the saloon where he could keep watch on both Bend Avenue and River Street. It was plain he didn't know they'd got the jump on us.

Maybe the exchange had already taken place? We'd been up most of the night making plans and slept later than unusual because of it. A surge of anger roiled up inside me. Chief should have just taken those royal baubles and been done with it! I should have insisted on it. But at the time it hadn't been my problem.

As I passed the marshal's office on the left, Marshal Bethany Bulger stepped out onto the sidewalk and called my name.

Since Bulger was in town and the two Mirratavia agents were not, I was even more certain now that she, Mace, and Hagmann had already made the exchange. I turned Blue Shanks to the hitching rail in front of her office.

"Decided not to run down those two men I told you about

last night?" She sounded disappointed, and maybe a little upset over it, too.

"There's plenty of time for that," I said easily. "Bill Riley had a year's start on me before I took after him." My view drifted up the street. Chief still hadn't looked my direction. "Sleep well last night?"

Her back stiffened. She hadn't, but she had no way of knowing I knew that. She said, "Your business is your business." She paused and hitched her head toward her office. "I got something in here I want to show you."

My guard went up, warning tingling at the back of my neck. "I'm in kind of a hurry, ma'am."

Her eyes took on a hard shine. "It won't take but a minute," she said sharply. "In here. Now."

The command reminded me of my mother's sternness when I'd disobeyed her. *Thomas Jacob Ragland. In the house. Now!* Old reflexes taking over, I dismounted and dutifully followed Marshal Bulger into her office . . . and stopped. Bobby Parker sat in the marshal's desk chair, wearing a deadpan expression that wasn't telling me anything as we looked at each other. Marshal Bulger crossed to the desk and lifted the heavy crowbar from it.

"Have you seen this before?" she asked, holding it out.

I took a calm breath even though my heart was pounding nails. "It's a crowbar," I said innocently.

"Very good. Go to the head of the class." She didn't sound pleased with my answer. If anything, her impatience ratcheted up. Those scum green eyes narrowed. "Let me be more specific. Have you ever seen *this* crowbar?"

I shrugged, pushing a smile across my face. "Well, to tell the truth ma'am, crowbars are a little like Injuns. They all look alike."

Parker said, "Let me help you out. It's the one I lent to last night." He stood and took a step toward me. "And its end matches the chisel gouges in Henry Hagmann's safe box."

There wasn't much to say after that. I could deny it, but they both knew it was true. "I suppose it does," I said and laid my cards on the table. "I suspected Hagmann had Bill Riley's head stashed in the box."

Marshal Bulger eyes widened. "And did he?"

"No. He has something more interesting in there. You know what it is, Marshal."

She gave me a green glare and let a breath slowly out. "That's what I was afraid of."

I said, "Breaking and entering is a crime, and I'll admit I'm guilty of that, but it's small change compared to stealing a royal crown and a pile of fancy jewels, not to mention the insurance fraud."

Bethany set the crowbar back onto her desk "How do you know about that? You never got the box open."

It was time for a little bluster. "I have my ways, Marshal."

She shook her head. "No. You have an accomplice. Who is he?"

So, she didn't know about Chief. He was still in the clear, and I was determined to make sure it stayed that way. "What makes you think so?"

She said, "I'll find out. Right now I have something else to do. We'll continue this later." Her view shifted, moving past my shoulder.

I knew then what it had been that had got my guard up. My hand reached for the revolver at my side as I spun about. And there I froze, staring at the big double bores of a two-shoot gun. Hagmann's face was behind it, looking tense and frightened. That's always a bad sign. Fear makes for nervous trigger fingers. Slowly I spread my palms and raised them into the air.

The gun gave a little jerk toward the jail cells. I backed into the nearest one and sat on the floor when ordered to do so. Bulger cuffed me to one of the bars. Parker's footsteps came up from behind me. Something soft and foul-smelling filled my mouth and was yanked tight and tied behind my head.

Hagmann exhaled hard. "This is going to cause big trouble, Beth. We can't let him go, knowing what he does."

"What do you suggest?" Bethany asked.

"It's either his neck or ours."

"Murder?"

I didn't like the sound of that, or the long pause that followed. Bethany spoke finally. "He had help. We need to know who it is."

Parker's said nervously, "I didn't see nothing."

"Nobody saw nothing," Hagmann shot back.

Bulger said, "You better leave now, and get rid of his horse on your way out."

Parker headed out the door without being told twice, slamming it shut behind him.

Bulger said to me, "We'll talk more when I get back, Ragland."

"Beth." Hagmann stretched that single word out into a question. "This isn't smart. Too much at risk."

Bethany said, "If you kill him here and now, we'll not find his accomplice, who likely knows as much as Ragland does."

I had an odd feeling that none of that really mattered to her. That what really mattered to Bethany Bulger was keeping me alive. I had to wonder why.

"Well?" she prodded.

Hagmann thrust the shotgun into her hands and turned away. Insurance fraud was one thing, but murder? He clearly didn't have the stomach for it. Neither one of them seemed to be up to that. She lowered the shotgun's hammers. I would have breathed a little easier if it wasn't for the foul-tasting rag that filled my mouth.

"I don't like it," Hagmann said again. "Too many people know."

"Too late to change that now." She looked at me with worry in those garish green eyes of hers. "Why didn't you go away like I told you?"

I didn't think she expected an answer, me being gagged and all, so I just stared at her, and she at me with something like regret in her eyes. With a grimace she looked away and said to Hagmann, "Close those curtains. Don't want anyone looking in and seeing him here."

She shut the heavy cell door, locked it, and dropped my revolver onto her desk. On her way out the back door she hung the key ring on a hook.

From where I sat, that hook might as well have been on the far side of the moon.

CHAPTER 16

Soon as they were gone, I went to work dragging the back of my head against the iron straps and ripped the gag off my face. It was a dirty bandanna they'd stuffed into my mouth—the same green one Bobby Parker had worn last night in his back room, building his trophy chest. I spat to clear the taste from my mouth, but it didn't do much to remedy the matter.

I considered my next move. The window and door were closed. I could have shouted for help, but that seemed the recourse of last resort. From inside my cage of checkerboard iron straps, I glimpsed my revolver amongst the papers on Bulger's desk. Like the ring of keys and the moon, the Remington might as well have been in St. Louis for all the chance there was of reaching it.

I gave the shackles a stout yank, more out of anger than any hope of breaking them. Bobby Parker's offer to buy Bill Riley's head that first night was beginning to look mighty good from where I sat now. I'd have been six hundred dollars ahead and on my way back to St. Louis . . . and Francine. It would have made good business sense for both of us.

I grimaced. No, it wouldn't have made good business sense for me, but it would have for Bobby Parker. Six hundred dollars would not be enough to satisfy Francine's father, but Bill Riley's head on display behind Parker's bar would bring in customers from all over. Once the word got out, riverboats would make regular landings at Bend City just so tourists could pay a visit to the Buffalo Wallow Saloon, take a gander at the famous outlaw, and buy a shot or two of watered-down whiskey. Parker would earn back his investment a hundred times over, and Bend City would prosper.

I felt a scowl pinched my face. Parker had the money in hand that first night, yet he had to hustle a loan from the Territorial Transfer Bank to pay for his whiskey shipment. What had happened to his six hundred dollars? Grimes had said Parker didn't gamble, so that's not where the money disappeared to. Grimes said that Parker only spent where he saw a return.

I gave the bracelet another angry jerk. All I accomplished was to hurt my wrist.

My thoughts switched tracks. Bulger said she had a job to do. The exchange? Had they not made the deal with those Mirratavia agents yet? Was the trade supposed to happen someplace out of town? Why? There were plenty of places in town to do it. Did Bulger want to do it out of sight so as to have better control over the exchange? Or . . . was it the agents who wanted to do it out of sight so that *they* could control the situation? Were they setting up an ambush? Was there a third agent no one knew about waiting downriver?

Too many questions filled my head, but the more I thought about it, the more that last idea made sense. King Frederick would have his crown jewels back . . . and keep the pay-off money, too. That would work out splendidly for a cash-poor kingdom struggling to keep its neighbors from scaling the castle walls.

I had to get word to Chief. Another yank on the cuff proved as futile as the first two and hurt my wrists again to boot. I reconsidered calling for help, but I wouldn't expect a law-abiding citizen off the street to free me, even if I could spin a convincing story as to why they should. Crown jewels? Train robbery? Foreign agents? A corrupt government official? Even I wouldn't have believed all that . . . well, maybe except for the corrupt government official part.

A sound pulled thoughts to a halt. I listened. All was quiet except for the ticking clock on the wall. And then there it was again: a soft *click, click, click* coming from the back door. I grinned. It was about time he got here.

Click. The back door opened slowly, and Chief crept in, scanning the place in quick glances. The sight of him filled me with relief, but I wasn't about to let him know that. I said peevishly, "It took you long enough."

He looked over at me huddled in the corner of the jail cell. A smirk moved across his face. "Behold the dangerous *hombre* who shot up the Riley gang."

"I'm in no mood for levity. Get me out of here."

"What happened?"

"Bulger lured me into her web, and Henry Hagmann brandished a shotgun in my face."

"Lured?" he asked, opening the flap to the grimy leather bag over his shoulder.

"Never mind." I wasn't about to confess to being swayed by a feminine voice and boyhood memories.

He took a pouch from the bag and began to unroll it.

I said, "It might be faster if you just use keys."

"Keys?" A whimsical looked came to Chief's face. "That's so old fashioned, Mr. Ragland." He shrugged. "Where are they?"

"On a hook by the back door. And hurry. The exchange may be going down even as we talk, and if I'm right, Bulger and her partners are in for a big surprise." In the few moments it took to open the door and free my hands, I told him what I'd learned and what I suspected.

I holstered my revolver, swept my hat up from the floor, and plunged out the back door saying, "I need to get a horse—" and stopped short, staring into Blue Shanks's nose. "Where'd you find her?"

Chief hooked a thumb over his shoulder. Bobby Parker lay in the alley alongside the wall. He was out cold.

We gathered Parker up, hauled him inside to the jail cell, and, feeling sweet revenge, I tied his own dirty bandanna about his head and mouth and snapped the cuffs about his wrists. Chief locked the cell door, tossing the ring of keys into a corner. On our way out he said, "I saw you coming up the street and stop to talk to the marshal—"

"You saw?" I interrupted him. "You weren't looking this way."

He pointed forked fingers from his eyes. "Me Injun. Me see everything," he said with a note of arrogance, as if that explained it all.

"Half Injun," I corrected. I was feeling bad enough as it was. I didn't need an uppity Injun, too.

"After a while when you didn't come out, I got suspicious. I couldn't think of any good reason for you to be visiting with the marshal, since you were only supposed to be keeping an eye on her."

I said, "She traced the jimmy marks on Hagmann's strong box to that crowbar I borrowed from Parker."

Chief looked amused. "Did you think your primitive attempt at burglary was going to go unnoticed?"

I shot him a narrow look.

He continued rubbing in the salt. "I've been into that lock-box four times, and no one's ever suspected." There was that uppity tone again.

"Well, mister smart-alecky, reckon you're just as clever as a hungry coon, aren't you? By the way, where's *your* horse?" Standing in the alley was only Blue Shanks, still looking annoyed at having to wear a saddle again and not having a bucket of oats and McGill's ready curry comb at hand.

Chief pretended he didn't hear my snide retort. "No time to get it. When Parker emerged from the building, leading your horse away, I knew you had got yourself in trouble and needed my help."

I winced, but he'd reckoned the situation true enough.

A look of satisfaction came to his face. "I had to act quickly, and with stealth. Unfortunately, Mr. Parker spent a while chatting with a passerby. Fortunately, when I was finally able to approach him, his curiosity was stronger than his sense of danger. I told him about the strange critter in the alleyway that I'd never seen before and wondered if he could identify it. He went to look at it for himself."

"Aha. The old critter in the alleyway routine." I swung up onto Blue Shanks's back, gave Chief a hand up onto her rump, and headed for Chief's camp, where his own horse was staked out near the riverbank.

A wheel track was our first clue, and, for all his Injun uppitiness, Chief rode right past it and would have kept right on riding clear to the Nebraska border if I hadn't seen it. To be fair, the road showed lots of wheel tracks. Finding some that drifted a bit off into the grass wasn't unusual, but this one was different. I swung to the ground.

Chief slipped off the back of his horse and came over. "What did you find?"

I pointed out the pair of wheel tracks in the grass. "They must not teach tracking at Cambridge." I was in a querulous mood because of Chief's arrogance, and maybe because of my embarrassment at having to be rescued by him.

"I missed that class." His view shifted my way. "I took a lesson instead on how to avoid getting handcuffed to a jail cell."

I ignored him.

We followed the trace a couple of rods off the road to where the carriage had stopped and then backed up to return to the road.

Chief said, "It appears they changed their minds."

"They must have been looking for something."

"A sign pointing to where they planned to meet up with their partner?" Chief ventured. He peered at the dense line of trees along the riverbank in the distance. "If your theory is correct and there was a third agent, he must have departed the steamer somewhere along here. Men from Mirratavia would not be familiar with the landmarks of this country. They would have arranged some sort of signal ahead of time." He looked back at me. "What sort of a sign might a third man have set up?"

"A signal fire or a flag might do. Maybe a blazed tree trunk?" There were only so many possibilities.

His lips scrunched to one side as he thought about it. "A stack of boulders? A branch set up as a post?"

"Or rocks laid out like a pointer?" I said, and we glanced at each other, having the same thought.

We spread out, searching through the grass, and found the marker not too far from where their wagon had come to a stop before backing up. Chief hunkered down and cleared away the dried vegetation from the stones. "These have been here a long time—too long to be their sign."

It wasn't really a pointer after all, just a dozen or so big stones someone had set more or less in a line. But it was obviously man-made, and it had caught the Mirratavia agents' eyes, making them stop to investigate.

We returned to our horses convinced we'd found an important clue.

Chief straightened the blanket and, grabbing a hank of mane, leaped astride his animal. "At least now we know what we're looking for."

"And that puts us ahead of where we began." I stepped into

the stirrup and swung up onto my saddle. We moved ahead slowly, scanning off the sides of the road as we went.

I had to wonder about Chief. He was an educated man—Cambridge, he'd said. So what was he doing running about the country chasing down insurance frauds? I didn't know anything about Cambridge except it was a highfalutin' school over in England someplace, and I seemed to recall that Sir Isaac Newton had something to do with it. A man with a Cambridge education surely could be doing better than Pinkerton's. "So, what lessons did you study when you were at Cambridge, Chief?"

Not taking his eyes from the side of the road he said, "Women, mostly."

I wasn't sure I heard him right. "Come again?"

Eyes still bent out along the grassy edge of the road, he said, "An Indian is something of a novelty in Great Britain—has been ever since Lady Rebecca arrived from the colonies and was treated as royalty. Turns out, women over there have this fascination with America's Indians . . . well, with the American West really."

I heard a smirk come into his voice. "Somehow I failed to mention to them that I was from Georgia. I gathered early on that their knowledge of US geography is wanting."

"You're a cad?"

He slid a reprimanding glare my way. "I'm no such thing. A cad is a dishonorable person. I was—" He paused to sort his words. "I was an item of interest."

There was more meaning in that than Chief wanted to talk about, so I moved on. "When you weren't being an *item of interest,* what else did you do?"

"I studied a little mathematics. That's a requirement of Cambridge, you know, a salute to the famous mathematicians of former times. Mainly I studied and read reams of English literature, and Greek and Roman, too. And I played a lot of cricket."

"Cricket?"

"It's a popular game over there, played with a ball and bat. The locals consider it an English institution."

"Like base ball?"

His view moved toward a distant wall of trees marching along the riverbank. "Not much like it except for the ball and bat. More like lawn bowling, with a little base ball thrown in for good measure. It's a lot more vigorous than either."

"Bend City is getting a base ball team together. Calling themselves the Bend City Injuns."

His head came around, his face wearing an incredulous expression. "Where'd you hear that?"

"Bobby Parker told me," I said, suddenly wary by his reaction. It made me wonder if I'd overlooked something. "Bend City has got something to do with some base ball association back East."

Chief gave a stinging laugh. "Who exactly are the Bend City Injuns going to play? There's not another town within fifty miles of here, and, even if there was, how would the teams get together for games? No railroad in this neck of the woods."

Dang that know-it-all attitude of his! The truth was, I hadn't given the matter any thought. I'd have forgotten all about it if Chief hadn't steered our talk toward the game of cricket.

"By steamer?" I offered lamely.

He laughed again. "What sort of timetables do steamers keep on this part of the river?"

I hadn't considered that either. When I admitted so, he lectured on. "You got to have regularly scheduled games for the national association to sanction a team. That's why you only hear of city teams like the Cincinnati Red Stockings, the Chicago White Stockings, the New York Nines, and the Knickerbockers. The national association isn't going to sanction a team in a backwater town somewhere in the middle of the Dakota Territory."

Chief was back to his annoying self again, and me, I was feeling an urgent need to take control of the situation. "Maybe they don't care about a sanction? Maybe they're only going to play for fun."

"Again I ask you, who are they going to play against? Bend City will have to make up two baseball teams and play each other." He huffed. "That will get stale in short order."

"Forget it."

We rode on, Chief looking smug and me feeling properly chastised. He began to mumble, talking to himself now, "Even if they did intend to *play for fun*, I don't think they'd find eighteen men in town who'd want to join."

"I said, forget it."

He glared at me.

I glared back at him . . . and then past him and drew rein. Off the side of the road stretched a straight row of newly laid down stones pointing directly toward a low hill beyond. The hill blocked our view of the river over that way, and of the carriage that had clearly turned off here. Its wheels had cut such crisp tracks in the dry grass, even Chief could see them.

CHAPTER 17

We swung wide, Chief to the south and me to the north. I lost sight of him almost immediately, and then I was in amongst the cottonwood trees. They grew thick here. I could hear and smell the river off to the east somewhere. Dismounting, I moved as quickly as I could through the thick timber, leading Blue Shanks because the trees grew too close to travel a'horseback.

The plan we had decided on was to come at them from two sides. Chief had particular instructions for me, and, since this was his show, I agreed to go along with them, even though I'd have planned it differently.

"If Bulger and the agents from Mirratavia are making the exchange," he'd said slowly, thinking it through as he spoke, "stay out of sight until they've handed over the jewels. That way you can serve as a witness later on. Afterwards I'll reveal myself to them. While they're being distracted by me, you come in from behind."

"And if the exchange has already taken place?" I asked, thinking that two of us moving in together would have a better chance, but, like I said, this was his show.

He said, "The plan stays the same, minus the witnessing part. I'll break cover and arrest the lot of them."

"You can do that? Arrest people, I mean?"

A devilish glint flashed in his dark eyes, and he patted the grimy bag over his shoulder in a meaningful manner. "I'm sure I can find something in here that says I can."

I shook my head in amazement. "You're a first-class snake oil hawker!"

"That's an improvement. A while ago I was a cad." His yellow teeth winked from behind a sudden grin. "Stay out of sight until I make my move. If it looks like it's getting out of hand, move in fast. It'll be a comfort knowing I have a backup."

"Do you think they'll roll over and play dead for you?"

He grimaced. "Probably not, but I want to give them a chance to do so." We'd left it at that and gone our separate ways.

By now Chief would be in position, expecting me to be ready to move in if he needed my help. I picked up my pace through the low, grabbing branches and broke out of the trees onto a narrow but well traveled trail along the river. Some of the hoof-prints looked pretty fresh. Bulger and Hagmann's horses maybe? We hadn't passed them on the road.

Climbing back onto Blue Shanks, I caught a glimpse of the brown Missouri River beyond the trees. Almost at once the trail widened ahead and spilled out on a small clearing. I dismounted again and gave Blue Shanks's reins a couple turns around a branch. I crept into the trees, going to a crouch a few dozen yards back from the clearing's edge.

The carriage McGill had sold the two men stood a little ways off, the horse still in the traces, grazing. I didn't see the agents, or Bulger and Hagmann. Thinking they might have wandered down to the river, I started through the trees in that direction. And stopped. Something on the ground on the far side of the carriage had caught my eye. It appeared to be a pile of rumpled cloth. As I studied it, the pile took on a shape. A second shape lay a little way off. My chest tightened. I gave the clearing another quick glance. Disregarding Chief's direction, I moved out cautiously, my eyes in motion.

I needn't have taken the precaution. There was no one around except the two bodies by the buggy. Both the Mirratavia agents had been back-shot. One of them had a big hole in his forehead, the back of his skull split apart like a walnut, gray stuff scattered on the ground. I got a little queasy in the stomach.

Chief's voice reached me from the direction of the river. "They're gone," he said, striding up the bank. He looked down at the bodies. "Pretty clear who bushwhacked whom."

"Both shot in the back. Bulger must have had someone here waiting for them. This one didn't die right off."

Chief didn't say anything for a moment but looked at the two. His head gave a shake, and he took in a breath. Like me, shock had seized his chest. We searched the carriage and then took a turn around the clearing, not finding the money or the crown jewels.

"What's the plan now, hotshot Pinkerton detective?"

My question caught him in the middle of a deep ponder. It took a second for him to pull himself out of it. When he did, his face had a puzzled look.

I said, "What does the Pinkerton instruction manual say about something like this?"

He clearly didn't know. Maybe there was no manual?

I said, "We can't leave them here."

Together we hefted the bodies into the back of the buggy behind the seat. I fetched Blue Shanks and tied her to the rear. Chief said nary a single word the whole time.

"You don't have a plan, do you?"

"Had not counted on this." Chief sounded faintly perplexed. He reached over and tugged on one of the agents' jacket to straighten it up some. His idea of a proper send-off?

I stepped up into the carriage and took the reins. "While you're working out what you want to do next, I'll drive these two into town. You best keep out of sight. Because you showed Bobby Parker that 'critter in the alleyway,' Bulger will know you're involved in this, too."

He nodded. I waited. When he didn't speak I said, "We know who has the jewels and the money. We know the players . . . well, some of them. Bulger, Hagmann, and Mace for sure. Parker knows something about it, but I don't think he's part of it . . . or maybe he is. Heck, maybe the whole town is in cahoots."

Chief said, "Now that's a thought. What are you going to do with these two? You can't dump them on the marshal's lap. Soon as she discovers you've broken out of jail she'll get up a posse and come hunting you. It'll be your word against hers, and this is her town."

"Who says I can't?" Something wasn't adding up. I didn't know what yet. It was only a nudging at the back of my brain, and I needed some time alone to work it forward. "I got a feeling we're dealing with an iceberg. Know what an iceberg is?"

"Cold," he quipped dryly.

"It's got a little bitty head poking above the water, and a big whale-of-a bottom hunkered down below. I think we're only seeing the tip of the head here."

Sudden interest shined in his dark eyes. "What makes you say that?"

"Base ball."

His head cocked to one side, a perplexed look on his face.

I didn't try to explain it to him, because I didn't yet understand what that whisper at the back of my brain was trying to tell me. "There's a trail back there in the trees. My guess is it follows the river to Bend City. It'll keep you out of sight should anyone care to look." I clucked the horse into motion.

Chief stood there watching me as I turned the carriage and rattled through the grass and up onto the dusty road heading back to Bend City.

Chief said I couldn't do it, but dumping those two Mirratavia agents on Bulger's lap was exactly what I intended to do.

Even so, I was in no hurry to get back to town. I needed time to work on the problem. Chief had been right. Bobby Parker had lied about a Bend City base ball team. But he hadn't lied about what he'd been building. It had looked sure enough like a display case, and by the careful effort he'd put into fitting the pieces together, it was going to be a fancy one at that.

If not base ball trophies, what had he in mind to display? The answer to that was plain as tracks across new-fallen snow to my suspicious brain.

Bill Riley.

What else could it be for? Surely not the Mirratavia crown jewels. Those would be sold off in some smoky Chinatown back room where buyers and sellers hide their faces behind paper screens.

Parker had wanted Bill from me that first night. Bill had been good for his business. I should have figured it out right from the start. I drove on, brooding over my situation. When I looked, the sky was beginning to darken toward evening. Maybe an hour or so of daylight left. The ride out of town and then back took most of the day.

I flicked the reins and put the horse into an easy trot.

Glancing back at the two bodies behind the seat, I suddenly wished I'd something to cover them with. Bodies don't generally bother me. I'd thought nothing about toting Bill Riley's head along in a gunny sack—except for the stink. But these two made me uneasy for some reason. I gave a short laugh. Did I expect them to rise up from the dead like some last day saints? Or was it Bend City's celebrated Injun ghost getting under my hide?

Chief claimed the yarn about Harel and Alice Lemuel's house being haunted was only an excuse for Mace to buy out the Lemuels' share of the jewels. He was probably right about that too—at least I hoped so. Still, I wished for something to cover them up.

Shadows were getting long when I rolled into town. I planned to drop these two foreign gents smack on Marshal Bulger's desk, expose her and Hagmann for the murdering scoundrels they were, and then march right over to the Buffalo Wallow Saloon and take care of business with Bobby Parker.

I had it all figured out . . . except that "murdering scoundrels" part. Earlier both Bulger and Hagmann had balked at the notion of killing me. How was it that these two men were different?

Up ahead a crowd was gathering in the street. At the sight of it, I drew rein, sitting there in front of Mace's hardware store, watching people drifting across Bend Avenue and along the boardwalk to grow the herd in front of the marshal's office. It was a pretty big gathering for a town hardly large enough to draw eight hale and hearty men to field even one baseball team. More than half of them appeared to be Injuns. If experience was anything to go by, at least half of those would be drunk.

It looked like Bulger was summoning up a posse and fixing to come after me and Chief. She must have known about Chief by now, for surely Bobby Parker had told her who had lured him into the alleyway to see the "critter." I ought to have skedaddled right then, but the more I studied the situation, the more I questioned the notion that this was a posse in the making. These folks there were just sort of bunched up like cows, peeking in through the door and past the window curtains.

A buckboard came around the corner from McGill's Livery, and as it drew up alongside the hitching rail, the crowd parted like those waters of old had done for Moses. Curiosity being an itch I couldn't reach to scratch, I eased the carriage up the street in front of the millinery shop and set the brake. No one noticed me, but with two bodies piled in back, one missing half his head, it wouldn't be very long.

My boots had just hit the ground when someone yelled, "There he is now!" The faces in the crowd turned, and two or three men detached themselves from among them and spread out toward me. I wasn't worried. I had my story and my proof in the back of the carriage, and, far as I could see, nobody had a gun except me. I strode boldly toward them.

"You got some nerve coming back to Bend City," someone said.

I turned in the direction of the voice and said, "Marshal Bulger is the one with the nerve, and I've come to see she gets her due."

My boldness caused just enough doubt to make them wonder. The crowd parted for me just like they'd done for that buckboard, and I shouldered through it and stepped around the heavy vehicle, hefting a leg to the high boardwalk.

I realized later that if I'd been smarter, I would have been scared. I wasn't. I had the goods on them, and I knew it. I was feeling bold, and, I suppose, a little vindictive, too, for being handcuffed inside Bulger's jail with Parker's grimy kerchief stuffed in my mouth. Now that I knew who'd done what, they were all going to get paid back in full.

Marshal Bulger came out the door carrying her shotgun. Without a moment's hesitation she shoved the gaping bores of that two-shoot gun against my shirt.

I sucked air.

Both hammers were cocked, her slim finger resting on the forward trigger. Having a big ten-gauge shotgun perched atop your heart is enough to freeze the air inside anyone's chest. "Hope you don't develop a twitch," I said tightly, eyeing the triggers.

"You do beat all, Ragland, showing up here after what you done. A man with any sense who done what you did would be

149

halfway to Wyoming Territory by now."

I shouldn't have been surprised she'd say something like that. Bulger was bluffing to save her own skin, and she had the town's people on her side so far. I said, "What have I done?"

"Try murder on for size." Bulger's timing was perfect, for at that very moment a woman across the street by the carriage gave a startled cry and pressed a gloved hand to her mouth.

A couple of men rushed over. "There's two dead men here," one of them said. With the help of an Injun and two white men, they hauled the Mirratavia agents from the back of the carriage and across Bend Avenue, setting them gently down on the boardwalk in front of the marshal.

One of them said, "These fellows' been shot in the back."

"I seen him come into town in that buggy," a creaky voice declared. I turned to discover the gray-bearded oldster from the saloon the first day I arrived in Bend City, jabbing a shaky finger at me.

Bethany Bulger stared at the dead men and then shot a fiery glare up at me, jabbing me hard in the chest with her scatter-gun. "You've been real busy, you bushwhacking bounty hunter. Is this how you caught the Riley gang?"

"It wasn't me who bushwhacked them, and you know it. It was you and Hagmann, and probably Mace. You did it so you could keep the ransom money and the crown jewels," I said loud enough for everyone standing there to hear.

Bethany Bulger's scum green eyes narrowed down to two slits, and a twinge of uncertainty hitched up the corners of her lips.

Someone in the crowd chortled. "Crown jewels?"

Another said, "He's been smokin' Mexican weed."

"Ain't thar a glass slipper missing, too?"

A low, uneasy laugh rippled through the crowd.

Well, it did sound kind of farfetched. I could see there wasn't much support for my position, and that made me nervous. I cast about for Chief, anxious for him to show up and back me. Evening was coming on, and I began to worry he might have decided to linger until after dark so as not to be seen coming back to town.

Although I was focused on Bulger and the shotgun jammed against my heart, something at the back of my brain was trying hard to get my attention.

There was some movement inside the marshal's office, and now a man came out and lowered the tailgate on the buckboard.

Gauging the general mood of the crowd, confidence returned to Bulger's face and showed in her voice. "Crazy talk about jewels and crowns isn't going to save your hide, Ragland." She glanced at a young man, really no more than a tall kid. "Carl, take his revolver."

Carl reached for my gun.

"Touch it, son, and you'll be a grease streak on this walk in two shakes."

The kid stopped right quick.

Bulger jabbed the shotgun hard enough to hurt. "You're begging for a hole in your chest, Ragland." She'd begun to sweat, and her cheek had developed a tremor. No one here would hold her to account should her finger twitch. She nodded to the youngster. "His gun."

Carl took a tentative step toward me. I stared at the nervous finger on the shotgun's trigger, and I let Carl take the revolver. He did and then backed away quickly.

She said, "You'll swing for what you done here today."

I said, "Without a trial? Without any evidence?" She knew I hadn't killed those men, but she had the upper hand. This was *her* town, and she had her own crimes to hide.

"I've got evidence enough, but you'll stand before a judge just the same."

I said, "I found these two down by the river and brought them in. Prove I murdered them."

"Not talking about these two."

That threw me. If not these two, then who? My confidence, already getting shaky, began to waver even more. I looked around quickly. Chief could back up my story and end this on the spot.

"Make way," someone called from inside the marshal's office. The crowd shuffled from the door as a man backed out holding onto a pair of legs. The legs belonged to a dead man. And then I saw his face.

Bobby Parker!

"You want evidence?" she said, her stare burning into me. Another sharp jab from the scattergun drove me up against the wall. "I'll show you evidence." She stuck out a hand, and one of the men leaving her office put my Bowie knife into it. "We found this in poor Mr. Parker's back."

The sight of the bone-handled Boyle Gamble blade drained the fight out of me.

"What's wrong, Mr. Ragland?" Her tone was snide, mocking almost.

"That thar's his Arky toothpick," the codger with the gray beard declared, his gnarled finger shaking like a twig in the wind. "Showed it to us when he told how he took down the Riley gang."

It was my knife, all right, the one taken from me the night Bill Riley's head got stolen.

I knew I hadn't skewered Parker with it, and, even more disturbing, unless I was reading Marshal Bethany Bulger all wrong, neither had she.

CHAPTER 18

The time had come to rethink what I'd believed to be true about Marshal Bulger, but the crowd was in no mood to give me that time. At the sight of Bobby Parker's limp body and the big officer's Bowie that had been extracted from his back, they riled up with blood in their eyes and vengeance in their hearts. Plainly Bobby Parker had been well thought of.

The buckboard rolled away, carrying the poor saloon keeper on his last trip to the undertaker's parlor down around the corner, and the people tumbled in behind it, hands grabbing. They threw me to the boardwalk and piled up on top of me so that I could hardly breathe. Fists and boots swung in from all sides. My arms were pinned back until my shoulders burned, and all I could do was lie there and take the punishment. Distantly, Bethany Bulger's shrill voice rose above their shouts, calling them off, but a fire had been lit, and it was going to take more than her yelling to put it out.

"Hang him!" was the cry from their throats.

And then a scattergun gave a mighty roar, and everything stopped. "There won't be any vigilante justice in my town!" Bulger shouted hoarsely.

"He murdered Bobby," shouted a voice I recognized as belonging to Irwin Wert.

Someone else said, "We'll give him a trial and then hang him."

That seemed to suit them. Immediately an angry roar

153

drowned out Bulger's protests. They hauled me to my feet, pretty near carried me across the street, and dragged me along with my boots thumping the sidewalk boards. It all happened in a blur of a moment. I was cast through a pair of batwing doors and thrust in a chair, and, when they finally backed away, I found myself sitting against a wall in the Buffalo Wallow Saloon.

Someone moved about the saloon lighting the lamps. Someone else slid behind the bar and began pouring whiskey. My cheeks burned raw and swollen, and my upper lip tasted of blood. Dragging a sleeve under my nose, it came away red. I gingerly tested my nose. It didn't feel broken.

They toasted the memory of Bobby Parker and then proceeded to select a jury. I don't think Bend City had anything like a real lawyer or judge, and at the moment I don't think that meant much to anyone except maybe Bethany Bulger. They'd hauled her along, too, and sat her in a chair near the front window. She looked genuinely distressed. Someone had taken her shotgun. Carl, the kid deputy, still had my gun, but he showed no interest in putting a halt to this kangaroo court. He must have been smarting over my remark about turning him into a grease slick.

Once everyone who wanted a drink held one, the fellow who'd fired up the lamps hefted a leg between crowded chairs and climbed atop one of the tables. "We need to elect a judge," he shouted, strutting around the table like a rooster. He gave a condescending nod to the marshal. "Gonna make this a proper and legal hanging, Bethany, just the way you'd have it."

"Nothing you're doing here is legal, Mr. Rawley," Bulger barked. "Turn Ragland over to me now and I'll overlook this . . . this . . . this circus of male stupidity."

I never thought being turned over to Bethany Bulger would be particularly appealing, but right then . . .

She was practically booed out of the saloon, except they

plainly wanted her there where they could keep an eye on her. They had no intention of letting her slip away and risk her throwing up a blockade to their stampede down the vengeance trail. Seeing her piqued face and hearing her incensed words, it was plain I might have misread her. My all-fired certainty that she and Hagmann had murdered the Mirratavia agents wavered greatly. If not them, then who?

The self-appointed ringleader strutting atop the table arranged for a hat to be passed round the saloon along with a pencil. Scraps of paper were ripped from the old Bill Riley wanted poster Parker had showed us the other night, and they began the jury selection process.

More men streamed in off the dark street, the barber, Boyd Nattingwood, and Doby McGill amongst them. Irwin Wert wore a nasty look as he came in and accepted a glass of whiskey. Injuns were sneaking in, too, taking advantage of the free liquor. I'd not spied Mace nor Hagmann yet, and *where was Chief?*

The faces of women too proper to enter the saloon floated outside the batwing doors like pale ghosts. I glimpsed Margaret Collins peeking in over the batwing doors but didn't see Franklin either outside or inside the saloon.

The men picked for jury duty gathered along the bar, having their whiskey glasses refilled. The hat circulated again, this time for selecting a judge. It seemed in Bend City they elected their judges the way some towns have raffles.

Somehow my hands had been overlooked and hadn't been tied. I wasn't being too closely watched either, except for a gent with a hand on my shoulder . . . but it didn't feel to be serious restraint, being that he was casting about for a whiskey like all the others were getting. Even so, my chance of escape appeared bleak. There were close to thirty men crammed into the saloon, not counting the Injuns sniffing out free drinks. Any chance of dodging past them looked pretty slim.

"Here's to Bobby!" someone proposed for the second time. Glasses clinked, and a thunderous roar practically lifted the ceiling. The nine jury members along the bar toasted to Bobby's memory with a gusto that didn't inspire confidence in their impartiality. The general level of sobriety within the saloon was plunging, I noted unhappily.

Still swaggering atop the table, the ringleader received the hat, turned his head aside in a show of impartiality, and ruffled through the slips of paper, extracting one. "Irwin Wert," he shouted above the din. Heads turned toward the batwing doors.

With a startled look on his face, the burly warehouse clerk turned a finger toward his chest.

"Yes, yes. You, Mr. Wert," Rawley said. "Come on up here and serve your duty to this here town. Declare this murderer guilty so's we can hang him and get on with our evening. I'm already late to supper."

Pushed along by helpful hands, Wert approached the table. As he passed by I could have sworn a glint came to his eyes and a small grin to his lips.

I glanced about for a way out of the saloon. There were only four. The front door. The back door through the storeroom. A small window that faced Bend Avenue—Marshal Bulger sat near that one. And another small window to my right, facing River Street. That one looked the most promising. With a running start, I could dive headlong through it, and if I didn't break my neck landing on the boardwalk outside, dash down to the river and swim like the deuces for the far side. I was a pretty good swimmer, and the darkness would make targeting me difficult should they take to shooting.

The self-appointed grand marshal of this here kangaroo court climbed down off his perch. "We need to clear this table," he told the men seated there.

"Clear another one," one of them said, and the other five

with him seemed in firm agreement. Thwarted, Rawley looked around for an appropriate bench for Judge Wert to roost upon. Not seeing anything not already occupied, he went behind the bar and came back with a three-legged footstool and set it right there in front of me.

"Here's your bench, Mr. Wert."

Mr. Wert, still staring at me, glanced at the stool. "It's too low."

Marshal Bulger shouted from the front of the saloon, "Enough of these shenanigans. Turn Ragland over to me, and let me send for a circuit judge. He can be here in a couple of weeks."

"Ragland killed Bobby," the ringleader said. "Bobby was a proper fellow, and his killer is going to swing."

"I didn't kill anyone," I said, half standing. The hand on my shoulder shoved me back into the chair. He was paying attention now that he'd found his drink.

"It's too low and undignified," Irwin Wert protested, staring down at the stool.

Exasperation sparked on the ringleader's face, and I sensed a rising desperation in him to get this over with. I got the feeling a lot of folks there were anxious for the curtain to come down on this playacting trial, but I had killed one of their own—at least so they believed—and there was a questionable notion of justice and the town's honor that needed to be upheld. And, too, there was the whiskey flowing free from the barrels newly arrived on yesterday's riverboat.

Rawley looked around, his view coming to a halt on me. "Get him out of that chair," he commanded.

I was pulled to my feet and my chair substituted for the stool, so that Mr. Wert would have a proper throne from which to conduct the proceedings. As they made the switch, the ringleader noticed my hands. "Someone tie him up."

That was the final indignity, and something snapped inside me. Untied, I had at least a chance at making a break. Tied up—well, that was a death sentence sure as tomorrow's sunrise. Quick as a scared snake I twisted out from under the hand on my shoulder, my fist coming up and cracking the jaw of the fellow at my side. He went down like a bag of wet sand.

Swooping low, I caught up the footstool by a leg and shattered it against the head of a fellow trying to grab my arms. Half the wooden seat went sailing across the saloon and busted the mirror behind the bar. One leg and part of the seat remained in my fist, and, as the men nearest to me began piling in, I commenced to swinging that remnant like Samson with his jackass jawbone. For the first few moments, the fury of desperation inside me made me invincible. I hacked my way toward the side window, men scattering left and right.

But their numbers were too great. Unlike Samson, I wasn't endowed with the Almighty's strength. Anger fueled by free whiskey had unleashed a mighty fury upon me, and I went down under a storm of flailing arms and kicking boots. When it was over, my hands were bound behind my back, and my nose was bleeding again. My side and spine ached, and my face burned like it'd been dragged through a cactus patch.

Jerked to my feet and slammed against the wall, the room tilted and swam in and out of focus. I staggered to stay upright. My vision cleared a little, but my ears had filled with a horde of buzzing cicadas, and the floor felt a little like the rolling deck of a ship in foul weather.

Those men sprawled unconscious were scooped from the floor and hauled out into the dark. Those who could still move under their own power scowled at me as they gathered themselves together to lick their wounds. Across the room Bethany Bulger was on her feet, hopping mad. I couldn't understand all of what she was shouting. What I did manage to make out amounted to something like, *Stop this travesty this very instant!*, although I think the language was a mite earthier, something unbecoming a lady, but I couldn't be certain past all the insects swarming in my ears.

Bulger was in fact as much a prisoner here as me; still, her words carried authority with some of the townsfolk. Tempers cooled a mite, and a few men drifted toward the saloon's door, shaking their heads in disgust, clearly not wanting to be part of vigilante justice, or its consequences once the territorial marshal down in Yankton got wind of it.

Bulger broke free and pushed her way forward. Not a man there dared stop her. She wagged a finger at the ringleader and declared, "Matt Rawley, I'll have your hide behind bars if you go through with this."

I surely was beginning to admire Marshal Bulger.

Rawley took a long swig of un-cut whiskey from his glass and said, "We'll hash this out later." His words had taken on a slur and his joints, a loose-limbed swagger. I hadn't been counting, but I was pretty sure I'd yet to see him with but a brim-full glass in his hand. A couple gents were making the rounds with pitchers, assuring that no one was wanting of a full glass. Even the Injuns. There was no discrimination tonight. The way I saw it, they were all stealing from the deceased saloon keeper . . . well, leastwise, from his surviving kin, if he had any.

Rawley shouted, "We're gonna do this, ain't that so boys," and the saloon erupted in agreement. I think he was getting a little worried and wanted to make certain his backside would be covered after the deed was done. He looked at Bulger. "Get back to your chair, Marshal."

Someone began chanting *hang him, hang him*. Others took up the drumbeat until the saloon rumbled with their voices.

I saw a change come to Bulger's face—a look of defeat, a loss of resolve. She might fight Rawley, but not all of them. Someone thrust a glass into Bulger's hand, and she tossed it back with hardly a wince. Right then and there I knew my case was lost. My last ally had joined the John Barleycorn lynch mob. With fading hope, I scanned the room for Chief. The place was thick with Injuns—but not Chief.

The warehouse clerk rapped his gavel, which was in actual fact the shillelagh Bobby Parker had kept behind the bar. As he called court into session, his eyes again took on an odd shine, the corners of his mouth slowly creeping up. "All you jurors come on over and pay attention now." From quiet and reticent to calculating and shrewd—I marveled at the change coming over him.

The nine fellows moved away from the bar and sauntered over, standing around me in kind of a half circle, some swaying on their pegs, a few grinning stupidly as they sipped their drinks.

Wert went on, sounding more sure of himself. "We got us a prisoner here, and it's our job to judge him innocent or guilty. Witnesses? We got any of those?"

"Don't I get a lawyer?" Plainly no one knew what they were doing. I wasn't much schooled in the ways of courts and juries and such, but I did know that much.

Wert looked exasperated. "Anyone here want to defend Mr. Ragland?"

No one stepped forward.

"I'll defend myself," I said.

Wert nodded. "Very good. That'll do okay." He seemed momentarily at a loss as to how to continue.

The whole scene was taking on a festive mood. The whiskey was doing its job, and few men there seemed to be much concerned over such mundane matters as protocol of a defense attorney. I was beginning to suspect if I delayed them long enough, I might walk out of there stepping over their drunken bodies. A couple of gents at the tables looked ready to keel over already, while fresh whiskey kept flowing into their cups.

I said, "I believe you also need a prosecuting lawyer, your honor." My jaw hurt when I spoke. My nose was still bleeding, but they had tied my hands so there was nothing to do about that but stand there dripping blood on the saloon's floor.

Rawley said, "Forget the formalities and declare him guilty."

"You're out of order," Wert barked, startling both Rawley and himself.

Rawley growled lowly, anger sparking in his eyes, but he held his words. It was a price to pay. As overseer of this witch-hunt, he was committed to playing it through to the end, even if that meant enduring a highfalutin' impetuous outburst from the judge. On the other hand, Wert seemed to be enjoying his brief flicker of fame and didn't want to see it extinguished too soon.

I looked through the crowd again, hoping for a sign of Chief. The Injun was nowhere to be seen!

CHAPTER 19

Wert called for a witness to the murder. Naturally, no one stepped forward. "We can't hang him if no one saw him do it," he said, a pleading tone to his voice. He really did want to hang me, and I wondered why. I'd never crossed him, at least not that I could recall.

"We got his knife," said one of the men who'd help carry Parker out of the marshal's office. He pushed his way forward and presented it to Wert.

Wert grabbed the bone handle in a tight fist and made a couple of plunging motions like he knew what he was doing. I recalled the thumping sound of him endorsing receipts with his rubber stamp the first time I'd met him. It occurred to me with some interest that the way he handled the stamper back then, and the way he handled my knife now, seemed almost second nature to him.

"And where was this found?" he asked as a matter of formality, since he'd been there in the crowd when they'd carried Parker to the wagon.

"Sticking out of Parker's back," the man said.

Maybe Wert had only wanted to hear it spoken aloud to strengthen the case against me. Or had he something else in mind? Wert looked at me with kind of an odd twitch to the corners of his lips, like he was playing some kind of game. "Is this your knife, Mr. Ragland?"

He knew it was, and I had no intention of going along with it and incriminating myself. "Am I now a witness?"

"You are," he said.

"The knife was stolen from me by whoever took Bill Riley's head."

Wert scoffed.

"It's his knife, all right," gray-beard said, wagging his gnarled finger. "He showed it the night he arrived. Told how he took off Bill Riley's head with it. It's a Confederate officer's Bowie. Said it'd been issued to him when he enlisted."

Someone in the crowd declared, "A Confederate officer? That man's a hero!" and he gave out with a rousing rebel yell that swelled my heart with fond memories . . . and some not so fond. A half-dozen other former butternuts joined in, pounding the tables with their fists.

As expected, a contentious scalawag shouted, "Hang the Reb!"

Some began to sing "Dixie," and some burst out with "When Johnny Comes Marching Home." For a minute or so the saloon rumbled with friendly banter and drunken emotions as battle lines were quickly redrawn along old sectional loyalties. It was all good-natured, but the festering scars of the war were still raw, and at any moment the gentle jabs might turn into rowdy punches. I hoped they would. An enthusiastic barroom brawl was just the cover I needed to slip away.

Rawley spoiled the fun. "Ease back, boys. You all can fight the war again after we hang this fellow!"

The blackthorn gavel pummeled the floor, and Wert called the court back into something resembling order. To my disappointment, the contentions settled down.

"This knife's pretty damning evidence, Mr. Ragland," Wert said severely, wagging his stick at me. "I don't need to see any more."

"Don't I get to defend myself?" It was only a show trial. I

knew that, and so did everyone else there, but it occurred to me there might be another purpose for these proceedings. In the morning, with clearer heads and heavy consciences, they could look back on it and lie to themselves that the hanging was all legal . . . if not a little unorthodox. Anyway, it was clear they were anxious to get the deed over with. On the other hand, I was anxious to draw it out to give Chief time to arrive.

A few scattered voices demanded I be given a chance to speak, Bethany Bulger's among them. Wert relented. "Go ahead, say your piece." He pulled a watch from his vest pocket and glanced at it. "Make it quick."

Cautiously, I stood away from the wall that had so far supported me. The ship's deck tilted a little beneath my feet, but the waves had calmed considerably. The faces peering at me from the scruffy sea of humanity packed into the saloon were a mix of boredom and concern. Most showed the dull expressions of men well along on their way to blurry-eyed drunkenness. I said, "I don't see a prosecuting lawyer. Who do I state my case to?"

"I'm the judge here. State it to me." Wert's face pinched, and his view narrowed. "You're tarrying, Mr. Ragland. Keep that up, and I'll bring down this gavel right now and declare your sentence." In his enthusiasm for getting me hanged, he seemed to have forgotten that there was a jury in attendance that would have the final say in the matter—at least they would have if this had been a real trial.

I studied Wert's fiery eyes, wondering about his all-fire zeal to have me dead. He twitched and glanced away as if ashamed or . . . or guilty?

A seed planted itself deep in my brain, and I had no notion what might sprout from it. I said, "When we left the marshal's office, Mr. Parker was alive." Immediately I knew I should have started differently, but the words were out of my mouth.

Wert latched onto that, and so did Bethany Bulger, judging by the way she sat up a little straighter in her chair. "We? Who else was with you?"

Chief was my holdout card. I couldn't risk revealing his undercover disguise, but I had to give Wert something to chew on, something to make him contemplate my innocence. I considered my answer before speaking. "His name is Robert LaCroix. He's a Pinkerton detective investigating the theft of a royal crown and a pile of royal jewels."

Across the room, Marshal Bulger scowled.

I said, "Marshal Bulger can tell you all about it, can't you, Marshal?"

Bulger said, "I have no idea what you're talking about."

"There he goes, babbling about crowns and glass slippers again. He's sure 'nough loco," someone declared and laughed, and the crowd picked up on it and bounced it about the saloon for a while.

Wert punished the floor again with the gnarled stick. When the noise quieted he demanded, "Where is Mr. LaCroix now?"

I took a long breath, shaking my head. "I wish I knew. We trailed those two foreigners south about five miles. Found them down along the river. They'd been bushwhacked. Shot in the back. I brought them into town, thinking it was the Marshal and Henry Hagmann who murdered them." I caught Bulger's worried look again. "But now I'm not so sure. I'm beginning to believe someone else murdered 'em, and I wouldn't be surprised to find out he's here in this saloon right now."

Wert's eyes bulged in his suddenly red face. "Ridiculous story." He furiously pummeled the floor. "Nobody believes any of this . . . this fairy yarn about magical jewels and golden chains!"

Well, his description stretched it a mite. I'd made no claim of the jewels being magical. But he was correct with the rest of it.

Wert said, "Men of the jury, make you decision."

They put their heads together for a powwow. It didn't take long. One of them staggered forward and hiccupped. "Whal, he's a likable fella, and he did kilt Bill Riley—"

Wert slammed the club down. "Bobby Parker was a likable fellow, too. Hang the murdering bounty hunter."

An almost spectral change had come over Irwin Wert. If I'd put any stock in such things as ghosts or demons, I'd almost suspect the man had become possessed. But I didn't, so it had to be something else . . .

There was no opportunity to puzzle it out right then. As soon as he'd said those words, a drunken mob descended on me and hustled me out of the saloon onto the dark street. I fought to shake them off, but I might as well have tried to shake off an elephant sitting on my chest.

The night had taken on a chill, the cooler air conjuring fog from the warmer river below and coaxing it up the hill in snaky, gray fingers that clawed along Bend Avenue, glowing in the light of a half-dozen lanterns held high to show the way toward Sawmill Road.

We passed the buggy still in front of the millinery shop with Blue Shanks still tied behind it.

Corralled by two dozen men, I was hauled up Sawmill Road in a cloud of intoxicated anger, past Harel and Alice Lemuel's abandoned house with its dark windows staring blankly out at us. I imagined seeing a flicker of light inside, but it was only a glint of moonlight peeking through long, tattered clouds scudding overhead.

The mob swept me onward toward the cemetery, where that big old cottonwood tree stood dark alongside the iron fence. Across the street a lamp burned in the window of the undertaker's shop. The wagon that had carried Bobby Parker's body was still out front. And then we arrived at the hanging tree. Someone commandeered the wagon and rolled it to a stop beneath the long, black branch that stretched out against the cloudy sky. A rope unfurled and came down, dangling above the wagon bed, a makeshift noose on one end, the other end tied off to the metal cleat affixed to the tree trunk.

In one last surge of desperation I tried breaking through the mob, but I only ended up driven to ground where fists and boots hammered me again. A dozen hands lifted me and tossed me into the wagon. I was hauled back to my feet and stood there swaying on the tailgate.

"Any last words?" This from the ringleader, Rawley.

Reality became fuzzy, like a blur before my eyes. "I didn't murder Parker," I said, tasting blood again, trying to steady myself.

Bethany Bulger's voice came from the crowd. "The territorial marshal will hear of this. You go through with this lynching, I'll see to it he knows every man's name who's here."

"Don't listen to her," Irwin Wert screeched. Maybe the devil really had taken possession of the man.

Rawley said, "Let's get this over with." The noose came over my head and was snugged up around my neck.

And then everyone got real quiet and solemn. I stood there looking out over that graveyard with its stark shadows shifting in the scudding moonlight, the river fog creeping in among the few tombstones and curling through the pile of rocks in the Injun part at the far corner. The fog over there seemed to take on a faint glow.

Realizing with a sudden shiver that this view was to be my last, I said a quiet prayer and readied myself to meet my Maker. I'd walked the sawdust trail at a tent meeting once, years ago when a preacher came through our town. Although I hadn't lived much of a religious life since then, I hoped my prayer

167

would go well for me when I stood before those pearly gates.

I felt every beat of my heart, every breath, waiting for the last one . . .

Someone said, "What's that sound?"

A murmur moved through the crowd. When I looked over, they were all glancing about. I heard it, too, then, a sort of *thump, thump, thump,* like a distant drum. The cadence was slow and regular, growing louder.

"It's a'comin' from back there where them Injuns are buried."

I'd located the sound and stared at the standing stones. They were kind of hard to see past the long tendrils of fog coming up from the river, but that faint glow I'd seen a moment ago was growing brighter.

The drumbeats stopped, the glow got more intense, and something moved. A wavering image rose slowly from the misty ground, faintly transparent and gauzy, like fine silk tulle curtains, the light shining as if from its very heart. The form was indistinct, but I judged it to be more man-like than animal, and it came forward as if walking on its knees—as if it was treading an ancient pathway now long buried beneath the sod.

The drunken crowd gave a gasp. "It's the ghost!" someone declared.

My breath made a lump in my lungs. The Lemuels' ancient Injun ghost story had been true after all.

A wailing screech pierced the night air. It sounded terrible. Brave men cried in horror as the apparition drifted closer, glowing in an unworldly way. Right then the crowd panicked. Like a human explosion, they scattered to the winds, tripping over each other like drunken sailors. Their wild flight spooked the horse, and the wagon lurched. I stabbed out a foot to try and keep upright, but the horse was on its way to join with the fleeing townspeople. The wagon rolled out from under me, my feet slipped off the end of the tailgate, and the rope went taut about my neck.

I was bound for Glory—and to meet that ghost on his own turf.

CHAPTER 20

It wasn't anything like a proper hanging where you march the condemned man up a scaffold to a trapdoor that opens beneath him, snapping his neck at the sudden stop at the end of the rope. The rope they'd used was too short, and my departure from the back of the wagon too slow. There was no fall, no snap, only a tightening about my neck as my boots slipped off the tailgate, and then I was swinging like a pendulum a couple of handbreadths above the ground. If the men all weren't so drunk, they might've arranged things correctly. But they hadn't. Instead of a neck-snapping jolt bringing on a quick death, the rope slowly tightened, closing up my windpipe sure as someone packing a handful of cotton bolls down my mouth.

I cursed my bad luck as I swung there, my lungs growing a fire in my chest, my eyes popping nearly clear of their sockets. I'd read somewhere that moments before you die your life flashes like a magic lantern show across your brain. Mine didn't. I just hung there like a sack of fish out of water, slowly suffocating. It was not a good way to die. I tried feebly to free my hands. The effort only tightened the rope further. I was getting more lightheaded by the second. My eyes blurred, but just before they did, I saw that not everyone had skedaddled. A few stood there watching, although I couldn't recognize a one of them.

I was passing out and welcomed the darkness. And right then that seed that had been planted in my brain during their monkey trial sprouted and shot a green shoot of revelation into my failing brain. In a flash, the pieces of the puzzle all came together. Unfortunately, the revelation had come too late . . .

Something grabbed onto my legs. At least that's what it felt like. I was too far gone to be sure. I did notice the rope loosening a mite from around my neck. A sudden whoosh of air surged down into my lungs, and then I was on the ground and breathing in huge gulps, and, oh, how wonderful that felt!

Something cold slid between my wrists, and my hands were free.

I looked up into the face of my liberator . . .

There was no face! No eyes, no mouth, just the gray ghostly shape hovering over me. I wondered if in actual fact I had died.

But then the ghost spoke. "Take deep breaths. You'll be okay in a few minutes."

The ghost had a voice I knew. "Chief?" I croaked, my own voice sounding huskier than I remembered.

The ghost grabbed me under the arm and pulled me to my feet. Bent low, we sprinted away toward the Injun grave stones. Well, the ghost sprinted. I just sort of stumbled behind it, being pulled along. We dropped behind the standing stones, and the ghost glanced around the edge of one of the larger ones. It said, "A few of the braver ones still hanging around. The rest crapped their britches heading for the hills."

Now I was certain it was Chief. I peeked around the stone, too. The crowd was gone except for a handful of people, looking startled and peering at the stones from across that iron fence. The sober ones, I mused. They seemed to be waiting for something, plainly in no hurry to follow us.

Chief worked at a knot and pulled what looked like sheer curtains off his head and shucked them off his shoulders. Beneath the outfit that brass lantern box he'd used in the fish works was tied round his waist. Its glow gave off enough light to see by. Chief tossed the ghost garb onto a nearby galvanized feed bucket fitted with a scrap of leather stretched over it.

I said, "Where the hell have you been?" The words hurt my throat.

"Nearby. I saw the whole thing—well, most of it." He blew out the lantern and folded the sides together, collapsing it flat. "Once it was plain they intended to hang you, I left."

"I didn't see you," I croaked, rubbing my neck.

"You wouldn't have, because I didn't want you to." That smugness had returned to his voice, but I wasn't annoyed by it. With the feel of that hangman's rope still raw about my neck I don't think anything Chief said could have annoyed me. He peeked around the rock again and then reached over and removed the noose from my neck, along with about four feet of rope. "Let's get out of here before they work up the nerve to investigate."

We leaped the back fence and dashed out into the prairie, lighting a shuck for the dark side of midnight. As we hurried through the tall grass, Chief said, "I staged that charade betting that in their drunken state their superstitions would overcome any common sense they might have had left."

"Well, it did," I said. *And mine, too,* I thought, but didn't say out loud. We traveled on until a low hill hid us from the lights of Bend City and then went to ground. I fell back in the tall grass, letting a shuddering breath escape my lungs, gazing up into the night sky. The stars peeking past the clouds glittered like specks of fairy dust. They were the prettiest things I ever saw—well, except for my Francine's bright eyes. I must have been lightheaded and kinda giddy about still being alive.

Chief's voice brought me around, reminding me there was work to be done. "I discovered something interesting on my way back to town. That river trace is a well-traveled path, but one sign stood out from the rest. A split hoofprint."

I said, "You followed it?"

"I did."

I sat up and brushed the grass bristles from my ears. "Let me make a guess. The hoofprint belonged to a mule."

I couldn't see his expression clearly, but his voice was suddenly wary. "I trailed it into town," he said slowly, as if urging me to finish the next part.

"And the trail ended on the wharf by the warehouse."

"How long have you known?"

"About five minutes." I grimaced. "It all came together as I was hanging there with that rope around my neck."

He said, "Where does that leave Marshal Bulger and her partners?"

"Up to their chins in insurance fraud, but not murder. There was genuine shock in her eyes when she saw those two dead agents. She really believed I killed them."

Chief thought that over. "If not her, then obviously not Hagmann or Mace either. So, who did murder those agents?"

"Try Irwin Wert."

Chief's eyes shifted back to me. I could see that he knew something, but wasn't sure he ought to tell me. "His name's not Wert," he said. "It's Turk. Sherwin Turk."

Turk? The name tickled a memory deep in my brain, but I couldn't recall where I'd heard it before. "How do you know?"

Chief's gaze narrowed a mite and then darted away. "I learned it while investigating this case."

"Is Turk in with them?"

"Far as I know, they don't know each other. But there is paper on him, and a reward."

My ears perked up. I'd lost Bill Riley's reward. Turk might be a way to recoup some of that money.

"He was involved in a shoot-out in Omaha—him and some buddies. He managed to escape. His friends weren't so lucky. It's kind of coincidental, him showing up in Bend City around the same time as Hagmann and Mace."

I frowned. I didn't like coincidences. They hardly ever played out as innocently as they sounded.

Chief said, "Brian Bulger and Bethany arrived a month or two later, after Brian somehow managed to get himself appointed a deputy territorial marshal."

"That makes for a convenient cover for the crime."

"If you can call it that."

"What else would you call it?"

"At most, they are guilty of being accessories after the fact. What it boils down to is, all they did was hold the jewels for Frederick. It's King Frederick who broke the law, but until I can prove it on this end, Lloyd's can't go after him on theirs."

I shot him a dubious look. "I don't claim to understand the legal particulars of all this, especially considering a foreign company and foreign laws are involved, but your definition of guilt sounds contrived at best and evasive at worse. At the very least, it seems to me a roundabout way to arrest a person, even if that person is a king."

"Technically no law was broken until Frederick filed a claim on the lost jewels. He did that in Mirratavia, out of US jurisdiction."

It didn't sound right. "After you prove Frederick was behind the theft, what are you going to do about Marshal Bulger and the others?"

"Nothing. They're of no interest to Lloyd's, so long as I recover the jewels and prove fraud on Frederick's part."

His answer was too glib. He was holding out on me. "Won't the territorial marshal back in Yankton want to—"

We both heard something move out there in the dark. A small nickel-plated revolver slipped quietly from under Chief's vest. My hand went for the Remington, and I remembered it had been taken from me by Bulger's kid deputy.

In the uncertain moonlight, Marshal Bethany Bulger came into view, not much more than a shadow with the shape of a shotgun cradled in the crook of her arm—not threateningly. "What you said sounded good to me, but is it worth more than just words?"

Chief glanced at me as if looking for insight into this woman. I only shrugged, as I was not in possession of what he wanted. Bethany Bulger was a puzzle I'd yet to gather all the pieces to. He gave a wry grin, and his reply held the faintest edge of caution. "You can take them to the bank."

"Put that revolver away. I'm not here to arrest you. We need to talk."

Chief hesitated, and then the gun disappeared back under his vest. "About a deal?"

"Deal?" She gave a derisive laugh. "No deal. You already said I was in the clear." She came closer and looked down at me. "A cat's got nothing on you, Mr. Ragland. I'm pleased to see you're still on the green side of the grass."

"Likely not as pleased as I am. I appreciate you speaking up for me back there."

She grimaced. "For what little good it did. Did you kill King Frederick's couriers?"

"If you thought I did it, that scattergun wouldn't be looking so comfortable there in your arm. Fact is, ma'am, I had intended to ask you the same question. It's clear now that neither one of us killed them."

"You really thought I killed them?" That seemed to startle her a little.

"I did at first. But after I saw the look on your face when their bodies were set before you, I started to have doubts."

She scowled, her view moving between me and Chief. "We seem to have a common problem, Mr. Ragland." Her gaze steadied on Chief. "You some kind of lawman? You don't look like one."

"Detective," he said briefly. I was glad he didn't elaborate. I didn't know how far to trust the marshal, and the less she knew about him and his peculiar bag of tricks, the better—at least for now.

She considered him a long moment. "Do I know you?"

He shrugged. "You've seen me about town."

"Hmm. Don't think that's it. Got a name?"

He started to speak but I jumped in ahead of him. "He answers to *Chief.*" I'd spoken his name earlier when Wert demanded who my accomplice was. Robert LaCroix hadn't sounded at all Injun-like, and maybe she'd not put it together. For the moment I wanted to keep her a little off-balance until I knew what she was up to.

"I found your costume behind the rocks. That was pretty clever, using Alice's old curtains to make yourself up like a ghost."

Chief just smiled.

I said, "Chief is full of surprises." It wasn't meant as a compliment, although I think he took it as one.

Bulger said, "Brian"—she glanced at Chief—"he was my husband. He worked for the UP shuffling cars at the Omaha switch yard, building up strings for the main line. One day a private coach was added into the queue. He was curious about it and put out feelers as to its owner. The baggage master told him it had been leased by a European dignitary. That same day there'd been a postal safe installed in the car. The baggage master had an ear to the ground and heard rumors that the foreigners were looking for partners in some scheme or another that they had up their sleeves. Brian let it be known he'd be interested in hearing more. Brian was working the early shift that day—he always got off early on Tuesdays. A couple hours later, at dinner time, two fellows showed up at our front door.

I said, "Those two foreign gents who ended up dead today?"

Bulger nodded. "They were blunt about what they wanted. It was not ethical, and, being a Christian woman, I was against it, but Brian saw it as a way out of the switch yards and into some easy money. This swindle had been planned from the moment they'd set foot in the States. They were on the lookout for willing accomplices."

I said, "How did the baggage master hear of it?"

"No telling how word gets around."

Chief had gone quiet, listening.

I said, "It seems your husband was in the right place at the right time."

Her lips tightened, and she exhaled hard. "Brian . . . he was getting desperate. You see, he'd applied for a deputy territorial marshal's job, and he'd waited a long time with no word coming. He was frustrated and looking for a way out of Omaha and the railroad business. Moving car all day long never suited him." She sighed. "But it was a living, and Brian was determined to see to it that I had a proper home and coal for the stove and oil for the lamps."

Chief broke his silence. "The boodle would have bought a lot of lamp oil."

"Eleven thousand dollars. Half a lifetime of working trains. Even split four ways, it was more than Brian could hope to make in ten years."

I said, "The split being Brian, Mace, Hagmann, and the Lemuels?"

She nodded. "Walter Mace worked at the Fullbright Mercantile. He'd been complaining for a year or more how he'd not been able to save a nickel. Harriman Fullbright was like that penny-pincher Mr. Dickens wrote about."

Chief said, "I read the book."

Bethany said, "Henry Hagmann had a fish salting operation along the river. Every spring the Missouri would rise up and take his business down. Sometimes for weeks at a time. That hurt him. He'd managed to get some lucrative contracts with the military, and when the river was up, he lost money."

I said, "I suspected he'd had some dealing with Mr. Missouri by the way he built his place here."

She nodded. "He said he'd beaten the river this time."

I managed a short, painful laugh. "No one beats the river, Marshal. They only put it off for a while."

"Harel Lemuel kept the books at Fullbright's. Same complaints as Mace. I can't say for sure, but I think both Harel and Walter were stealing from Fullbright's business, feeling they deserved more than Harriman was willing to pay."

Someone was coming through the grass—maybe two or three by the sound of them.

Bethany lowered her voice. "Didn't take them long to screw up their courage and get curious."

I took Bethany by the arm, and we crouch walked away from there, swinging wide of the town silhouetted against the moonlit waters below. Once out of earshot I said, "How did all of them get involved?"

Bethany said, "It was easy money, but Brian didn't want to do it alone."

Chief said, "Spread the blame, spread the shame."

She shot a look at him as we made our way through the dark toward the back side of Bend City. "Something like that." She sounded annoyed by Chief's remark. "Fact is, they were all looking for a way to break with Omaha. Hagmann had found a buyer for his business, and he and Mace—they're cousins you know—had already made plans to move to the territory."

Chief said, "I didn't know that."

We looked at him. There was no reason for him to have

known. That he made a point of mentioning it at all seemed curious. I said, "Your investigation didn't turn up that fact?"

He cleared his throat. "No."

Bethany looked at him with a piercing intensity that set my neck hairs bristling. "You sure we haven't met?"

A smile like oil on water spread across Chief's face. "I would certainly remember meeting such a lovely lady as yourself, Mrs. Bulger."

Bethany's jaw went slack, and that put an end to that subject.

I said, "The baggage master, what was his name?"

"I never knew it. He wasn't part of Brian's circle of friends like the others. I think he'd only just begun working for the UP when this all came about."

"Could it have been Wert, or whatever he called himself back then?"

"Irwin Wert?" She shook her head. "Don't be silly. I'd have recognized him right off if he was the same man."

We came to the edge of town and halted behind the Big Muddy Café near where I'd rooted up the Collins's vegetable garden. A lamp lit the upstairs window. That reminded me that I hadn't seen Franklin earlier at the trial.

Bethany Bulger said, "It's all got out of hand. No one signed up for murder. I have a bad feeling those two emissaries will only be the beginning if we don't end it now." She looked at Chief. "Who you working for?"

"Pinkerton."

She said, "You're Mr. LaCroix, the one Ragland mentioned?"

He nodded, and that bird was out of the nest. So much for me keeping Bethany Bulger off balance. She was too clever to be unsettled for very long.

"Thought so. You come for the jewelry no doubt?"

Chief said, "And the money. Lloyd's paid off the insurance claim knowing they'd been bilked. So now they want to get the goods on King Frederick and recoup their losses—and those losses include the money the Mirratavia agents paid you and your partners."

"You get that, and we're off the hook? Right?" She didn't sound convinced. She'd heard what he'd said earlier, and, like me, it sounded off to her. I didn't blame Bethany for moving ahead cautiously. If Chief was lying, it could mean jail time for her and the others.

"All Lloyd's cares about is Frederick. He's the one who defrauded them. They, in turn, hired the Pinkerton Agency to provide evidence of fraud, not to round up everyone who might have been involved. Like I told Ragland: the fraud was committed in Europe, not America."

She looked at me. "That true?"

"It's what he told me."

That seemed to put her more at ease with what she was going to do next. "All right. I'll take that as your pledge, Chief." Her view hitched toward me. "And I will expect you to cover my back should your Indian friend double-cross me."

"He won't." I gave Chief a look meant to warn him he'd better uphold his end.

Bethany said, "The money's in Henry's strongbox."

"And the jewels?" Chief asked.

Her face pinched angrily. "We kept our end of the bargain. Frederick's couriers had them when we parted ways. Find their murderer, and you'll find your fancy loot."

We circled wide of the town and came around to the wharf near the place Chief had his campsite. Hagmann's Fishworks building stood off a little way, dark and looking gangly on its stork-leg stilts. No one seemed to be about. We crossed River Street and ducked under the building, moving carefully amongst the pilings. Chief's fancy folding lantern would have helped, but the light would have given our position away.

We made it to the back loading platform unseen, and Chief started to untie his roll of lock picks.

Bethany reached past him and tried the handle. The door swung open a few inches. Something was wrong. The three of us sensed it. Hagmann was not one to leave doors unlocked.

Chief drew his revolver. Bethany pushed the door all the way open with the barrel of her shotgun. The building was dead quiet. I wished I had my revolver as we crept inside and past the skinning tables and salting tanks.

Bethany grabbed the sleeve of my shirt and pointed.

The door of Hagmann's strongbox stood open.

Chief whispered, "We're too late."

I started forward. My foot hit something lying on the floor.

It was Henry Hagmann.

CHAPTER 21

I seemed to be running into dead bodies a lot lately. I shouldn't have been surprised at finding another one now, but bumping into the mortal remains of Henry Hagmann in the dark, in a place I wasn't supposed to be, summoned up an extra beat to my heart, and a sharp gasp that might have been an embarrassment if the sight of Henry Hagmann lying in a puddle of his own blood had not aroused the same startled response from Chief and Marshal Bulger.

Bethany set her shotgun aside and went to one knee, rolling Hagmann onto his back.

Chief moved to the window and peeked out while I did a quick search of the place, including the dangling forest of dried fish in the back. The murderer wasn't here. He did what he came to do and then left in a hurry, not bothering to lock the back door behind him. My pulse began to return to normal.

"He's dead." Bethany glanced up, her eyes wide in the faint moonlight. "Poor Henry." She turned her palm toward me to show me something that I couldn't see, but I knew what it was. "It must have just happened. The blood's still warm."

Chief came back and hunkered down beside Bethany. "All quiet outside. No one heard the shot."

"That's because there was no shot." I grabbed the handle of the knife and gave a tug. It didn't come out easy. In his death spasms Hagmann's stomach muscles had clenched like a fist around the blade of a thin filleting knife.

182

Chief grimaced. "Hard way to go."

Bethany stared at the knife. "Someone in Bend City is mighty fond of cutlery." Her throat sounded tight, but she managed to steer clear of any emotion, just making it a plain statement of fact. She went quiet except for the harsh sound of her slow, deep breathing. There was history here—Hagmann, Brian . . . and Mace. In those few long seconds she might have been remembering how it had been back in Omaha before all this began. And she might have prayed some, too. She seemed the sort of woman who would do so.

Whatever it was that had taken hold of her thoughts, she let it go, and that was just as well. I didn't need Bethany Bulger grieving over Henry Hagmann, no matter how long they'd known each other. The bodies were piling up. Four of them already today. I didn't want emotions to make her careless and raise the body count by one more.

She looked up at me, a wet streak on her cheek. "Let's get Henry out of here."

"Not yet."

Her view swung back toward me showing flinty anger. "We can't leave Henry here, in his own blood."

Anger was a good sign. It meant she could put aside the grief long enough to tend to the problem of finding the murderer. Hagmann was dead. He didn't care where his body spent the next hour or two. I didn't tell Bethany that. Like I said, there was history. So I made it sound reasonable. "It's better if whoever murdered Henry doesn't know we're on his trail just yet."

The hardness left her face. "You think you can follow the bastard?"

"I won't have to, so long as we don't spook him."

She regarded me with suspicion. "You know who did it?"

"Not for certain. Ever since the sham trial and that rope

around my neck, I've had a strong hunch. But there's still one other person."

"Who?"

"When you and Hagmann met those two agents and made the exchange, was Walter Mace with you?"

She looked puzzled, and then indignant. "You don't think Walter did this? They're cousins!"

"Did he go with you?"

She exhaled sharply. "Walter stayed behind to keep an eye on you and find a way to keep you here in town should you get nosy."

"Well, he didn't do a very good job of that. Have you seen him since you made the exchange?"

She thought a moment and slowly shook her head. "Come to think of it—"

Chief said, "It appears someone is shutting down a pipeline."

I nodded. "I think we ought to check in on Mr. Mace."

"What does he mean, pipeline?" Bethany asked.

I said, "It means we may already be too late."

We were too late.

This time the murder weapon hadn't been a knife. Except for all the blood, the hatchet looked brand new, like it had just been taken off the store shelf and used only this one time.

Bethany turned away from the sight of Wally Mace crumpled in the narrow hallway at the foot of the stairs. There was a quiet sob, but she wasn't going to let us see her like this.

Chief stepped over Wally Mace and crept up the stairs to the rented rooms above, revolver in hand. He returned in less than a minute.

"No one up there. The door to the outside is unlocked."

"Mace never locked it. Only ever locked this one to the store."

I indicated the door to the main floor, which stood open. It'd been open when we'd discovered Mace.

We left the store by the back door that spilled us out into the alleyway, across from that leaning Methodist Church. It was near here where I'd awoken the morning after Bill Riley's head had been stolen. Thinking it over, I was mighty lucky not to have gone to sleep permanently, with a knife in my back—my own Bowie.

Bethany hadn't spoken. Maybe she was thinking of the friends she'd lost tonight? Maybe she was thinking about Brian? She walked out of the alley's shadows and stood on Sawmill Road, peering down past McGill's stable at the dark river below.

I started toward her. Chief caught my sleeve and said quietly, "She's the last one."

I hadn't thought about it like that. First it had been Brian Bulger who, according to Bethany, had died a few months after coming to Bend City from a fall. And then Harel and Alice Lemuel leaving town a few days ago, before all the bloodshed began. Today it was the two Mirratavia agents, Bobby Parker, Wally Mace, and Henry Hagmann. That left only Bethany who knew what had happened back in Omaha. If someone was in fact shutting down a pipeline of witnesses, Bethany would be next.

Another thought occurred to me just then. Bobby Parker's murder didn't fit the pattern. He hadn't been a partner in the jewelry fraud, and he hadn't come from Omaha. He'd come from Chicago.

Other than Parker, the common thread tying them all together was Omaha. "Come on, Chief." We left the alley, hauling Bethany Bulger along with us. She'd have plenty of time to grieve later. Right now we had a murderer to catch.

The three of us hurried along the boardwalk. If anyone still had any interest in hanging me, they didn't show it. The lynch mob members had found their ways home or were passed out in a gutter somewhere. Most of the buildings fronting Bend Avenue were dark, and no one was out and about on the street. Maybe they'd all been spooked by Chief's ghost charade and really believed the town to be haunted after all.

The saloon door was still open. I pushed through the batwings and was stopped by the sight before me. I'd not lived a sheltered life; I was no stranger to saloons; but I don't think I'd ever come upon a scene like the one inside the Buffalo Wallow Saloon.

The overhead lamps were guttering. No one was tending them. Some had gone out. The broken mirror behind the bar reflected the fading light in dim, splintered rays. Scattered about the place lay the remnants of a free-for-all that had followed the trumped-up trial. Scraps of papers littered the floor. Shattered furniture poked up here and there like broken bones. Whiskey glasses had been crushed under foot, making dark streaks across the floor.

The place looked like one of General Sully's Injun wars—red and white bodies cast about as if they'd fallen in battle. Some sprawled across tables, some on the floor. A few were folded across the bar. I was pretty sure they were all breathing, although come morning, plenty of them would wish they weren't. Those slumped in chairs and still clinging to an appearance of wakefulness didn't seem to notice us come in. Maybe me thinking they were awake was too generous? Whatever passed for vitality amongst them had taken the last steamer down river and was long gone.

Bethany stepped in behind me, her foot crunching on a fragment of glass. The sight stunned her, too. I couldn't read her expression as she looked around. After finding Henry Hagmann and the gory mess that had been Walter Mace, all this ought to have been mild by comparison . . . or was it the final piece of straw settling into place? I didn't know Bethany Bulger well enough to know which way this sight might go with her. What I did know was that she hadn't chosen to be a lawman. The job had been plopped hard into her lap. That she had carried the weight of it for this long spoke to a certain amount of steel in her spine. She was a remarkable woman, and I wondered in a vague manner how my Francine would have fared had she been forced into Bethany Bulger's shoes.

I realized I was frowning.

"I'm glad I'm not the one who has to clean this place," Chief said flatly, looking around. He moved off to the left, stepping carefully as he wove his way through the few tables. I moved to the right, scanning the floor.

Bethany stood there a moment longer. "What are you looking for, Ragland?"

I spotted a scrap of paper and picked it off the floor. It was all that remained of Bill Riley's wanted poster, the one that had been torn into small slips and used to select the judge—Irwin Wert.

I handed it back to her. "More like this."

She looked at the scrap of paper, puzzled. "Wanted posters?"

A familiar shape in the corner caught my eye. My knife! Probably skittered there during the brawl that had plainly taken place some time after the lynch mob had marched me down the street to the local hanging tree. I fetched it up with sudden joy. Me and the knife had been companions for a lot of years together.

By now Chief had worked his way around the saloon to the bar. He slipped behind it and hauled out a bunch of posters all rolled together. "This what you mean?"

We made our way across the battleground, stepping over bodies, dodging a breastwork of broken chairs and tables. I dragged one of the fallen heroes off the bar and set him in a corner where he could sleep it off without being stepped on.

Chief unrolled the posters. There were maybe eight or ten of them. The one I was looking for was about midway through the bunch. Chief held one corner of it while I flattened it out on the bar. Bethany moved closer and studied the face. The name printed under it was *Sherwin Turk*. The price the Omaha Police Department figured the fellow worth for someone to go to the effort of returning him to them was only eight hundred dollars. I'd have considered the amount an embarrassment had I been Turk. Given enough time and a little effort, the bounty was likely to rise. Maybe it already had. It was, after all, an old poster, as Parker's copy of Bill Riley's poster had been.

The face would not have been familiar if I didn't know what to look for. The artist had done a fair job. It wasn't his fault Turk had changed his appearance since the sketch had been made. "Recognize him, Marshal?"

"No. Should I?"

"Take another look. Maybe you might have seen him in Omaha from time to time?"

Chief's lips shaped a smirk. He saw where I was heading.

Bethany looked doubtful, but she gave the poster a longer, harder study this time. Her bright green eyes narrowed. "There might be a small resemblance to the man from the coal company who filled our bunker every month."

"Do you recall when the man would come by? Was he on a regular schedule?"

She was becoming impatient. "This better be going somewhere, Ragland. It would have been a Tuesday. He always came the first Tuesday of the month, unless we sent for him in between like we sometimes did in the winter months."

It'd been a long shot. More guessing on my part than any solid evidence. After years of running down desperadoes, you develop a knack for it. Some guesses even pay off. I said, "That's all you recall?"

188

Her face pinched. "I'm in no mood for games, Ragland. Who is this man, and why should I know him?"

I began searching under the bar, peeking in tins, pulling open the drawers of a mechanic's tool box. "Do you recall what day of the week it was Prince Frederick's agents showed up at your door?"

"How would I remember that?"

I looked up from my searching. "I believe you mentioned it just a while ago."

Her head tilted. "I did?"

It had been a long day, and the particular unpleasantness of it enough to blur anyone's memory of an incident that happened almost a year earlier. "Think back, Marshal. You said Brian had got off from work early."

The fog lifted. "That would have been a Tuesday. Brian always worked the early shift on Tuesday."

I found the piece of thick, black crayon Bobby Parker had used the other night to make a quick window sign.

"And what happened every first Tuesday?"

Her eyes gave a green flash of anger. "Don't quiz me like I was a schoolgirl." She looked back at the picture of Sherwin Turk and stabbed a finger on his nose. "He came by in the coal wagon."

I turned the poster and went to work on it. "Might Sherwin Turk have been at your house filling the coal bunker the very Tuesday Frederick's agents arrived to talk a deal?"

"It's possible. And in answer to your next question, it's possible he overheard them making plans, too."

I finished sketching a black, bristly beard on Turk's chin. For someone who'd never laid claim to any artistic talent, it was a fair effort. Good enough to do the job.

Bethany stared at the transformation the addition of a beard had made to Sherwin Turk's face.

"Irwin Wert."

CHAPTER 22

The saloon's storage room door stood half open. A strong odor of whiskey emanated from back there—stronger than I recalled from my earlier visits, but it was too dark to see anything.

Turning up the wick on one of the lamps from behind the bar brought the struggling flame to life. I pushed the door wider with the toe of my boot, thrusting the lamp ahead of us. The place had been ransacked, but not like a drunken mob might have done. There appeared a method at work here. Kegs of whiskey had not been toppled off the shelves but had been moved about, relocated from where I'd helped Parker stack them the day before. Parker had been pretty exacting as to where he'd wanted us to place them. There didn't seem a good reason for him to be moving them again afterwards.

The trophy case he'd been building still lay upon the sawhorses as I remembered it from last night. Chief looked it over, running a finger over the mitered corners. He seemed to appreciate the craftsmanship even if he didn't say so.

Bethany stepped around it, stopped, and lifted a shoe, frowning. I moved the lamp to better see what she'd stepped in. Whiskey. A lot of it, and recently spilled, too, seeing as little of it had dripped through the spaces between the boards yet. I said, "Check if any of these barrels have been broken open."

We did a quick search and found only one cask with a tap in the bunghole. It wasn't leaking, so we looked a little further.

Bethany called us over to a cask in a corner lying on its side with its top removed. "Unless I'm much mistaken, cutting off the top of a barrel isn't how Mr. Parker would get at his whiskey."

Chief said, "It would indeed be an unorthodox method of getting one's whiskey out of a barrel."

She scowled at him. "What's religion got to do with anything?"

I said, "Chief's got more words inside his head than a schoolmarm's speller. Don't encourage him."

He gave a smug grin. The Injun was a peculiar critter, but that was his problem, not mine. He helped me lift the cask out of the corner and set it upright. There was still some whiskey inside. I held the lamp close to the keg as our heads came together over it.

Bethany said, "What are you two looking for?"

"A clue," Chief said, sounding now like a detective instead of a dictionary.

"A clue to what?" Bethany was becoming peeved.

We said, "Bill Riley" and looked at each other. We'd both caught hold of the same idea at the same time.

She looked puzzled and then shook her head as if to clear the confusion from it. "In a whiskey barrel?"

I said, "I've looked everywhere else I could think of."

Her head joined ours over the barrel. "What sort of *clue* are we looking for?"

Chief said, "I will know soon once I find it."

She reached inside the barrel. "You mean something like this?" And drew out a couple long strands of coarse, red hair.

I said, "That's Riley, for certain."

She said, "What's he doing in a whiskey cask?"

I had the urge to say that Riley always did have a strong affection for the stuff, but I refrained and said instead, "Being pickled, I suspect. So that he'd keep a long time in Bobby

Parker's trophy case."

Chief said, "What better place to hide the evidence until Ragland gave up searching and left town?"

She said, "It was Mr. Parker who slugged you and stole the bounty head?"

"No, that would have been Irwin Wert, or Sherwin Turk, if that's indeed his real name." I cast a questioning look at Chief.

He rolled his shoulder. "Who knows what his real name is? The nice thing about the territories is you can become whoever you want to be."

The way he'd said that raised a warning inside me. "A drunken Injun or a Pinkerton detective?" I suggested.

A little smile came to his lips. "Exactly."

Bethany was still pondering the Parker/Wert conundrum. "Why did Parker have the head if Wert stole it?"

All I could do was speculate on an answer. "Once word got around that I had Bill Riley's head in the saloon, people started arriving from all over town to take a look at the infamous outlaw. For a while, the Buffalo Wallow Saloon was doing a booming business, and Bobby Parker nearly ran out of stock to serve. You see, his shipment hadn't arrived on schedule."

"Whatever does?" Bethany said, rolling her eyes in exasperation at the steamboat companies' inability to keep to a schedule along the Missouri River.

Chief said, "Parker offered to buy the famous head off Ragland. Turk overheard the offer."

I said, "How do you know that?"

He pointed to a corner. "I was standing right there."

"I never saw you."

"You didn't see me because I didn't want you to see me." He'd said it again, and with that same arrogant tone and superior smile. I'd let it pass the first time, but it irked me this time around because it'd been a while since I played the guest of honor at a hanging jamboree, and the bite of that rope around my neck felt a mite more distant now.

"So Turk waited for me to leave the saloon," I continued irritably. "He knew everybody and their brothers were pushing drinks on me, including Parker. When I wasn't looking, Wert—er, Turk—bushwhacked me with a blackjack and took Bill Riley and my knife."

Bethany said, "Why take the knife?"

"I was sorely drunk and unsteady on my pegs, so I'd tied the cord around my wrist to keep from dropping the bag. I figured that way if I fell, I wouldn't lose it. I suspect Wert had trouble getting it off and grabbed the knife nearest at hand."

Chief said dryly, "It's a wonder he didn't just cut your hand off."

I said, "Maybe he was in a good mood."

Bethany's eyes narrowed in a speculative way. "You're guessing at all this, Ragland."

"I am, but it seemed mighty strange to me that when Parker's whiskey arrived on that steamer, he hadn't the cash to pay for it when just a couple days before he'd offered me six hundred dollars to buy Bill Riley. That got me to thinking. How had Parker spent so much money in that short of time? The only thing I can think of was that he'd bought something mighty expensive. A bounty head maybe?"

She said, "Let's say you're right about all this. What's Wert's next move?"

Chief said, "You're the last person left who can tie him in with Omaha and the two murdered agents."

Her sudden change of expression showed she understood what that meant.

I said, "And afterwards, he'll shuck this town just as fast as I can. He'll have a bounty head worth three thousand, the ransom money worth another eleven thousand, Parker's six hundred, and a bundle of jewelry worth . . . what?" I glanced at Chief. "You said an appraisal came in at two hundred thousand dollars, if I recollect."

Chief nodded.

Bethany whistled softly, which is generally regarded as unbecoming a woman of culture, but she had a lot of other redeeming qualities. Being a woman of culture was not all it's been made up to be, I decided. Maybe I was growing a little fond of the feisty marshal of Bend City?

Chief said, "So long as he believes he's still in the clear, he'll very likely wait until the next steamer arrives. All he has for transportation right now is a lame mule. After today's exercise, I do not think that ass is going to want to be walking anywhere soon."

I wasn't so sure Chief was right about that. "He has two other choices," I said. "He can walk, or he can get a horse from McGill's livery stable. In either case he'll be easy to trail."

Chief thought that over. "Now might be a good time to see that we don't have to trail him."

"He lives in an apartment at the back of the warehouse." Bethany started for the door.

I said, "Give me the shotgun."

She straightened her spine. "I'm the law in this town, Ragland. I'll keep the gun." Her face softened a bit. "Well . . ." She leaned the gun against the door jamb, unfastened the top two buttons of her dress, and turned demurely away from me, reaching inside. She came back around and placed a tiny Remington derringer in my hand. It was warm and smelled faintly of lavender toilet water. "It's all I have on me right now."

My admiration for her was growing. I broke the action on the derringer and checked the chambers. The brassy glint of two rimfire cartridges showed in the lamplight. I hefted it and gave a wry grin. It wasn't much of a pistol. A .41 caliber derringer might discourage a man if he wasn't serious and you waved it in his face, but if you had to actually use it, you'd better hope he wasn't wearing a heavy coat or carrying a wallet in his breast pocket, or even a gold watch in his vest. Even a stout leather belt might stop a bullet from one of those pigmy smoke poles, but it was probably better than a clenched fist in a fight. And it had been her hidey gun, and I appreciated having it.

"Thanks. It's still warm."

"Ragland!" She sounded appalled that I'd noticed and quickly cinched up her open dress. I'm not sure—the light wasn't all that good—but Bethany Bulger appeared to have worked up the makings of a blush.

CHAPTER 23

Bethany tried the back door to the warehouse. Unlike the fish works, it was locked. There in the dark alleyway she looked at me. "It appears we will have to use the front door."

"Not to worry," I said. "We've got this covered."

"We have?" She sounded skeptical.

"Chief, it's all yours." I took her by the arm and stepped back.

He unfurled his roll of lock picks, selected two of them, and thirty seconds later eased the door open. The hinges were well oiled, letting us slip inside the pitch-black building unheard. There was not a hint of light anywhere.

"Where did you learn how to do that?" she whispered, impressed.

"Don't ask. You'll only encourage him."

Chief laughed softly.

I said quietly, "Where's the apartment?"

"I don't know. Never had a reason to go there."

Chief snapped together his little magic lantern and lit it. The clever contraption must have been fitted with a daguerreotype filter because the light that showed dimly from it now was red.

"Be careful not to bump anything," he said starting forward.

We stalked about the place like pirates until we came upon the door to Wert's apartment. After a moment or two listening for sounds on the other side of it, I gingerly tried the knob. The door opened a crack, and the smell of a recently snubbed candle came from the gap. He'd gone to bed. Maybe still awake? Maybe about to blast some holes through the thin wall? My breath stilled, and the hammering of my heart pounded in my ears.

Chief took a step backward, out of the line of fire. I moved Bethany quietly to one side. If Wert began shooting, he'd be aiming at the door where we huddled.

Chief took another step backward. It turned out to be a step too many. There was a thump and then a crash, followed by the ringing clatter of pipes falling upon each other. Chief's fancy lantern skittered and disappeared beneath the landslide.

I pushed Bethany aside and hit the floor, her baby pistol pointed at the door. Out the corner of my eye Bethany backed deeper into the shadows, out of the line of fire. I hoped she had sense enough not to use that shotgun with me so close to the door.

The rattling clatter died down, and Chief's low groan came from the darkness. He could wait. Wert would come investigating any second. When he didn't, I knew we were too late. Bethany made her way to the door and pushed it open with the barrel of her shotgun.

Those pipes began to clang as Chief moved, untangling himself from the mess. At least the landslide hadn't broken his neck or knocked him unconscious.

Bethany inched forward. I rose, sprang to the other side of the door, and, bent low, dove inside. The room was empty.

"He's gone," she said.

"He was here not long ago." The smell of the smoldering candle was still strong. Maybe he'd only gone out to the privy, but I didn't think so. Irwin Wert/Sherwin Turk had fled Bend City and with him went the gold, jewels, and Bill Riley's head.

I dropped the derringer into my pocket, found the candle, and put a match to it. The shelves on the wall of the tiny apartment were bare. The blankets had been stripped from the tick mattress. He'd left some clothes behind in his rush to vacate the place. We went to check on Chief and found him sitting on the floor, looking dazed, but all in one piece. Lengths of iron pipe lay in a pile all about him like a bunch of giant toothpicks.

"He's not there?" Chief asked, stating the obvious.

"Looks like Mr. Wert had a sudden urge to leave town," I said. "He's taken the whole caboodle with him."

Massaging his knee, Chief said, "He knew we were on to him."

"Or maybe he figured with me still alive and him having set me up for that hanging, I'd be hunting him. He had what he wanted. Probably figured it smart to leave while it was still dark."

Chief tried to stand and fell back.

"You okay?"

"I don't think anything's broken. Feels like I wrenched my knee. Give me a hand."

I got him to his feet. "Give the knee a rest. We'll hit his trail in the morning. He's either afoot or on muleback. Either way, he won't get very far."

Bethany said, "There's another way, Ragland."

I shot her a look that made her flinch.

"Wert keeps a boat tied up at the pier. It has a canvas cover over it most all the time, except when he takes it across the river to deliver hardware to the sawmills on that side."

This changed everything. There's no easy way to trail a man on water. He'd be long gone by morning.

Chief cut loose with a burst of colorful language and took off in a hobbling gait toward the big doors. I passed him by in a couple of strides. The wide freight doors had been left open enough for a man to pass through. Wert had no intention of coming back, so why bother locking the place up? I plunged out onto the wharf and stopped, Bethany right there alongside me.

The low moonlight painted the wharf in a pale gray light and glinted on the river as if someone had cast the shards of broken mirror out across the water.

Bethany pointed. "There he is!" At the far end of the pier Irwin Wert stood inside his boat, bent over, not looking our way. She didn't wait for a reply.

I was right on her heels, and then she was on mine.

Hearing pounding of my boots, Wert swung around from whatever he'd been doing and lunged for the bow line, casting it off. The boat shifted in the current, rotating away from the pier as he scrambled over the lumpy tarp toward the stern line still tied to a piling.

I'd crossed most of the distance between us, and I would have beaten him to the stern line if he hadn't pulled out a revolver. In the dark, the muzzle flash stabbed a long, orange flame in my direction. I flinched aside and dove to the deck. Wert fired again, missing me again. Behind me Bethany gave a grunt, staggered, and fell.

Wert had the stern line off the piling. It slapped the water, and the little boat began to drift, stretching that rope out behind it as the current took the boat away from the pier. I hesitated, glancing between Bethany and Wert. It was an agonizing decision, one I didn't want to make. It sort of made itself. Wert had murdered five men today, and that was plenty enough by any count.

Leaping back to my feet, taking two long strides to gather speed, I hit the edge of the pier running and sprang out over the dark water. Momentum carried me . . . not far enough. My boot found the edge of the boat's gunwale, and I came down on it with all my weight. The boat pitched sharply, casting Wert headlong into the lumpy tarp. The revolver flew from his grasp and skittered away along the dark bottom.

I teetered on the gunwale, making crazy gyrations in a desper-

ate attempt to regain my balance. And then I lost my struggle with gravity and pitched over backwards into the river.

We were still close enough in to the bank that my feet found the muddy bottom not far below water. Bracing myself, I stood, gasping in a breath. Something swooped out of the dark. I ducked back under the water as the oar skipped along the surface where my head had been. It would take a few seconds for Wert to set up for another swipe. I counted and stood again, ready for him this time. The man was predictable, I can say that for him. The oar came back around as I suspected it would, and I grabbed for the shaft. Although I couldn't catch it to stop it, I did manage to get a momentary grip on it, enough to pull Wert off balance. He was already wobbly, posed as he was at the side of the leaning boat. He lost his balance and hit the water, arms flailing.

I was on him before he went under, and I knew at once that I had caught me a real wildcat. He'd shoveled coal and moved freight most of his life, and he had built powerful muscles in his arms and back to prove it. He threw me off and drove me back underwater. Trying to fight like that was sort of like trying to fight your way out of a big cotton boll. The water made everything move like in a bad dream where you run hard and get nowhere. I tried to kick, tried a punch. Wert didn't seem to feel anything; he just held me in those powerful vise-like grippers of his. He didn't have to fight me. All he had to do was keep me down long enough for my air to run out. Already my lungs were feeling a burn.

I braced my feet against the bottom and tried to lift him. That worked enough for me to break the surface and steal a breath of air. We grappled with each other, and then he had me down under the water again. I took a swipe at his leg, hoping to knock him off balance, but he stood firm. I grappled at his wrists. The burn came back. I twisted and tried to push off the

201

bottom again. He'd figured that one out already and was ready for it. There comes a time when desperation takes hold of your thinking. When that happens, you've lost the fight. I fended it off, trying to think clearly while I was still able to do so. Fighting him wasn't getting me anywhere. Wert was stronger than me. Fighting him on his own terms would be my undoing. I did a quick inventory. My hands were free. I had a knife, but I couldn't reach it at the small of my back, and then I remembered the derringer.

Managing to get a hand into the pocket, my finger wrapped around the piece. I prayed that the shells had remained watertight as I cocked the little hammer and pressed the stubby barrels against Wert's belly.

Underwater, a gunshot sounds more like a thump than a bang. Wert lurched back.

Free from his grasp, I shot for the surface and gulped in a glorious lungful of air, shaking the water from my eyes. Wert stood off about five feet, his hands underwater somewhere in the vicinity of his stomach. He wore a look of shock, but that was only momentary, for the next instant shock turned to rage. The bullet had hurt him, but not bad enough to stop him. He lunged at me like a wounded bear full of fury. I was ready for him this time. I moved forward to meet his charge and with what strength I had left drove the big Bowie knife below his ribs. The knife went in deep and hard, and I gave it an upward thrust. His heart and lungs were there, and the Bowie found them. Wert toppled like a puppet whose strings had been cut.

My breathing was coming in rasping gasps. I felt weak but managed to hold on to him. Three men had died at his hands today by a blade of one kind or another. I figured, in a distracted way, as I hauled him through the water toward the boat, the Fates had meted out proper justice on Irwin Wert, or Sherwin Turk, or whoever he had really been. I ought to have let the river take the body away and the catfish strip its bones, but he had an eight-hundred-dollar bounty on his head, and I had no intention of letting that sink to the bottom with him.

The boat had drifted downriver, towing the mooring line behind it on the dark water. Snagging the trailing end of it, I reeled the boat back against the current and, not without a little effort, heaved Wert's heavy body inside it. Afterwards I stood there, elbows hooked over the gunwale, breathing heavy, giving my strength a few moments to return. I spied there on the floor of the boat a small chest that had sprung opened. The graying sky to the east cast a faint dawn light upon the crown and jewels. A little exploring uncovered another box. A familiar stench, tinged with a strong odor of whiskey, brought on a grin. I'd found Bill Riley. I opened the box, gratified to see Bill's death mask snarling up at me. On a whim, I placed the royal crown on Bill's tangled, red mop.

"The coronation of Bill Riley. From outlaw to royalty." I laughed. "Well, they were about one and the same . . ."

And then I remembered Bethany.

CHAPTER 24

Five minutes is a long time for a gun-shot person, long enough to die.

The killing of Irwin Wert hadn't taken but a couple of minutes, although while I'd been about the task, it had seemed a lot longer. Hauling the boat back to the pier and tying it off again had taken another minute or two at the most.

Chief was kneeling at Bethany's side by the time I reached her. I went to my knees beside them.

"Turk?" he asked.

"Dead. How bad is it?" I was uncertain what I was seeing in the weak dawn glow.

He shook his head. "I don't know. Lots of blood."

Bethany was in shock. Her eyes were open, staring, and her gaze moved slowly toward me.

Chief removed his hand from where he'd been putting pressure on the wound. The bullet had gone in low and to the left, most likely collapsing a lung. Her ragged breathing seemed to confirm that. There was lots of blood, but it wasn't spurting. That was a good sign. It meant the bullet had missed the heart and hadn't cut a big artery.

"I need to get her to a doctor."

"In Bend City?" Chief sound skeptical.

"There's one in town." I carefully took Bethany up into my arms. Beneath all the petticoats and the folds of her dress, she felt smaller, lighter than even her slim appearance had suggested. I hitched my head at the boat, strung out at the end of the rope. "Your crown and gold are there, and so is my bounty head and Wert."

Chief nodded. "I'll take care of it. You take care of the marshal."

I don't recall the trip to the barber shop. I ran most of the way, and if it winded me, I wasn't aware of it. The barber shop was closed this early in the morning. I burst it open in stride and rushed inside, calling for Nattingwood.

I heard someone stirring about up the stairs. Boyd Nattingwood came cautiously down them wearing a gray, plaid nightshirt and armed for bear. When he saw me and Bethany, her dress soaked in blood by now, his eyes went wide, and he set the shotgun down on the stairs and hurried over.

"She's been shot," I blurted before he had a chance to ask.

"Lay her there." He indicated the hospital bed against the wall.

I did and then moved aside. He began cutting away at the dress while I stood there weak-kneed, something like a big clock spring winding tight in my stomach.

"Light a lamp, and bring it here," he said, not looking up.

I was thankful to have something useful to do, confused by the urgency I felt for Bethany Bulger, by the panicky rush of my breath and the hammering of my heart. I'd seen bullet wounds, blood, and death lots of times. How was this different? I didn't understand it.

"Put a fire in the stove, and get water to boiling."

I didn't have to be told twice. The stove was in the back room where once, a thousand years ago, I'd soaked in the big copper bathtub, dozing over old newspapers. That seemed so long ago now. Had it something to do with those puzzling feelings?

The stack of old newspapers was still where I'd left them, as if no one had looked at them since I had. I was about to wad up a couple of sheets when I saw that the piece I held was the very one where I'd read about the missing royal jewels. I folded it into my pocket, starting the fire with the rest of the newspaper.

By the time I got back out to the main room, the sun was up, and morning light filled the shop. Nattingwood had Bethany's upper body exposed in a way that ought to have embarrassed me but didn't.

"How is she?" I asked, careful not to crowd him.

"Lucky," he said briefly.

A little while later I carried over a kettle of hot water and fetched some more towels off a shelf, a roll of bandaging material, and a bottle of phenol from a drawer. Then I paced the small shop a while, and when I looked again he had cotton gauze pushed into the wound and another pad under her. Still a lot of blood, but that was only appearances. He'd got most of the bleeding under control.

"The bullet went clean through," he said giving me a glance. "I didn't have to dig for it."

That was good news, but her breathing was still coming hard. "Cut the lung?" I asked.

He nodded.

I knew that likely meant it had deflated, and that she was struggling to get by on one lung.

When he'd finished, Bethany lay on the bed covered up to her neck with a sheet, still breathing hard. Her eyes were open, alert, and they moved toward me when I stood over her. Those eyes had taken on a deep green color, like the emeralds in King Frederick's coronation crown. We just looked at each other for a moment, and then I swallowed down a knot in my throat and said, "Does it hurt?"

She almost laughed, wincing back the effort. "I was about to ask you to this Saturday night's dance on the town square."

Well, it had been a foolish thing to ask, and I deserved that. I managed a smile. "Bend City doesn't have a town square."

She took a shallow breath. I saw how it hurt. "So much for that idea." Her view shifted, and she stared up at the tin panels on the ceiling. "Wert?"

"Dead."

"That was my job, Ragland."

"Yes indeed, ma'am, and if you hadn't stepped in front of a bullet, I'd have let you do it."

"Liar." That used up about all the strength she had for talk.

Nattingwood's flannel nightshirt was blood stained. I was pretty well covered in blood, too. He said to Bethany, "Looks like you're going to cheat the undertaker this time." His voice was deep, rich, as I remembered it from the first time I'd met him, and he seemed right pleased with the prognosis.

She swallowed a couple of times, working up strength. "When can I go home?" Her eyelids were growing heavy.

"Not so fast, Bethany. You're still bleeding. I'll see about rounding up a litter and a couple of men, and maybe tomorrow we can move you." He looked down at himself and frowned. "I'll just run upstairs and get dressed."

"I'll sit here with Bethany," I said dragging a chair around.

"Don't have to stay," she managed.

"I want to."

Nattingwood went upstairs, collecting his shotgun from the stair tread along the way. When I looked back at Bethany, her eyes were closed and her breathing a little lighter, not so labored. Sleeping was good for her now. I sat there a while looking at her and then became distracted by the rustle of the newspaper in my pocket. Having staked my place here at her side, and with nowhere to go for the moment, I removed the paper and re-read the story about the jewel theft. It all made sense now in a sort of convoluted way. The only picture with the story was the woodcut print of the baggage agent. Looking at it now, the face was somehow familiar—the shape of the eyes, the lips . . .

Suspicion began to gnaw a hole in my chest. Frowning, I went hunting up a pencil and caught one on the counter behind the barber chair. Quickly I sketched some long, tangled hair on the picture and then stared at a familiar face peering out at me from the line-cut drawing.

Chief!

He was long gone by the time I made it back to the wharf, and so was the boat, the gold, the jewels, Bill Riley, and eight hundred dollars' worth of bounty money being offered for Irwin Wert/Sherwin Turk.

I don't know how long I stood there at the end of the pier staring down that slow, muddy river, hoping I was mistaken, waiting for Chief to reappear around the river bend paddling hard against the current. But I wasn't mistaken. Chief never came back.

A sudden ruckus over at the fish works pulled me from my gloomy numbness. Injuns and white men had begun scurrying about. They hauled Henry Hagmann's body out of the place, and I'm pretty sure someone went for the marshal. It wasn't but a few minutes later that a second hubbub arose south of the wharf, up Sawmill Road somewhere in the vicinity of Wally Mace's hardware store.

It would be a busy day in Bend City today as its citizens sorted out all that had happened. I grimaced and slowly strolled back down the pier to the wharf, thinking about the loss of all that I'd worked so hard for . . . and Francine . . . and her stern father. He'd never allow us to marry now. The weightiness of it all dragged me down even lower. I tried to shake off my despair. I told myself firmly that I'd just have to work doubly hard now to win Francine's hand. I'd have to find some occupation that would position me in a way that would please both her and her father.

Pondering all this, my feet took on a mind of their own and carried me along the riverbank to the place Chief had built his campsite. Everything was as I remembered it from last night. Even his horse was still there, tethered to a tree on a long lead. With the toe of my boot I nudged the tilted coffee pot in the pile of gray ashes. I bent for a tin sitting on one of the fire ring stones, opened it, and winced at the disgusting smell. Heaving back an arm, I pitched it far out into the river.

Chief had been in on the swindle from the beginning. He'd been good—very good. No one had suspected him, while all the time he'd hung around right there under their noses. I'd been swindled along with the rest of them, but at least it'd been done by a first-class mountebank. Curiously, that made me feel a little better, but not by much.

Chief had made off with over two hundred thousand dollars' worth of booty. I didn't feel at all bad taking his horse to McGill's livery stable and selling it for twelve dollars. I collected Blue Shanks along the way. She seemed pleased to see her stall and oat bucket again.

Afterwards, I went up to my room, changed my clothes, and went looking for something to eat. A sign in the Big Muddy Café's window informed me the place was closed. I got the feeling this was a permanent situation.

Eventually I found my way back to the barber shop to sit with Bethany.

Later that afternoon a steamer from up north arrived at the landing. It took on wood and some passengers, I was told, and went on its way—without me and Blue Shanks. Somehow, getting down to Fort Leavenworth didn't seem all that important anymore.

CHAPTER 25

I hung about town on the pretense that Bethany might need my help. She didn't. The ladies of Bend City had circled the wagons, seeing to it that she got fed and bathed and generally coddled like woman folk tended to do. In actual fact, I was stalling because I hadn't figured out my next move. Slowly, over the days, a plan began taking shape in my mind.

After about a week, Bethany was moving around under her own steam. She was one tough gal, and I favored that about her. She might have been up on her feet, but she wasn't moving very quickly, and it obviously hurt her to walk. Her walking slowly got better over the next few days.

Sometimes we'd stroll side by side along the boardwalk, me steadying her by the arm. She didn't need the support, but she didn't refuse it either. During our walks I'd not infrequently talk about Francine, and her father's demands, and tell Bethany of my plans to get my lost bounty money back. I'd already decided I was going to hunt down Chief like I'd done Bill Riley and the four or five men before him. She would listen, not saying much except now and again to ask a question or two. The questions were always shrewd and probing, and most of the time answering them in an honest way felt a little like a too-tight collar I might wear to church, or to one of Francine's fancy soiree musicales she was fond of hosting.

"It's not so much the price you need to concern yourself with but the cost of upkeep," she'd said once for no reason I could reckon. I didn't know what to make of that. We'd been talking about me needing to sell Blue Shanks to McGill to get up enough money to buy passage downriver.

As I got to know her better, I became aware of little things I'd not noticed when I first arrived in town. Sometimes while walking along the boardwalk, she'd stop and peer into a plate-glass window at a display beyond. At first I thought that was all there was to it, but then I saw she was really looking at her own reflection. She'd maybe touch her hair, or the ribbon that often held it in place, and then frown as if displeased at what she saw and move on.

I couldn't figure out what she might be displeased about. She wasn't hard on the eyes—not lovely, like my Francine, but easy enough to look at and easy to be with. I never commented on it. Just thought it curious.

Another curious thing. Bethany had lost the bluster I'd noted upon our first meeting. Was that because she wasn't trying to prove anything now? Or maybe knowing that just two inches to the right, and Wert's bullet would have killed her, had made her introspective. A part of me missed the old Bethany, but, in truth, I was liking the new Bethany more and more.

Then came the day the steamer *Paxton* arrived. I'd seen the smoke-smudged sky far up the river, heard her steam whistle drifting down the water. There had been other steamers before her, of course. I'd let them pass on by, but now I knew the time was right to move on. Chief had a good head start on me. I wasn't too worried about him. Bill Riley'd had an even greater head start, and I'd tracked down his trail and run him to ground. I'd do the same to Chief and then make like a scalded chicken back to St. Louis and my Francine. In my musings, I'd see her rushing from her father's big city house with open arms, I'd feel her strong embrace, and then I'd see Pierre Toutant's stern face melt as I pulled $3,800 out of my pocket.

It pained me to give Blue Shanks a final pat on the neck, and she knew it was good-bye, too.

"I'll see she's well taken care of," McGill promised.

"I know," I said, my throat tight. I gathered my things and turned my back to her. Blue Shanks tried to follow me out the barn, but her halter rope pulled her up short. I should never have looked back into her big, brown eyes. A lump filled my throat and hurried out into the bright sunlight—so bright that it stung my eyes and made them wet.

Last thing in the world I wanted to do was sell that horse, but lingering in Bend City had left me flat broke. I'd bought supplies and food on credit and had to pay them off before I left town. Blue Shanks was all I had worth selling, other than my revolver and rifle. But old Blue, she was worth more than both, and I didn't know how long it was going to take me to catch up with that thieving Injun.

Sadness weighed heavy on my chest as I trudged along the boardwalk carrying my few belongings, making my way down to the wharf and the steamer that would take me away from this town.

And good riddance! I grimaced.

My steps got heavier as I turned the corner and took in the sight of the big, white steamer docked at the end of the pier.

It ached to be leaving without saying good-bye to Bethany and a few other friends I'd made in my time here in Bend City. *Leaving would be easier this way,* I told myself, a little perplexed that leaving ought to be difficult at all.

"Is this the one?" Bethany Bulger said from somewhere behind me.

I turned and spied her standing near the warehouse. She crossed the few feet between us, moving carefully but with no sign of having taken a bullet through her ribs not quite three weeks earlier. I was pleased to be able to see her one last time, even though I'd convinced myself I oughtn't be.

"The longer I wait, the more miles Chief puts between me and him."

"You might not catch him. Then what?"

It was a possibility—one I'd not wanted to consider. Too much was at stake for me to not find him. "I have to," I said briefly, only half aware of the buzz of activity all around us.

Bend City's wharf was a sleepy place until a steamer arrived, and then the river front became a confusion of activity—people gathering together, cords of firewood being hauled aboard by broad-shouldered Negroes, cargoes being off-loaded or carried aboard. Today not much in the way of cargo was going aboard since the fish works had closed down.

The warehouse had a new clerk, presently consulting a clipboard with one of the boat's crew. Just inside the warehouse's big doors stood a stack of nail kegs. The pile had grown over the weeks, as no one had come to claim them.

We started walking toward the pier, Bethany at my side as she had been all these weeks of her recovery. Her being there felt comfortable.

She said, "What will Francine do if you show up with empty pockets?"

"It's not so much Francine as her father."

Bethany thought for a moment. "When you marry a woman, the in-laws come bundled with her. It's like buying a ranch. You not only get the prancing filly, but all the cows, too."

I laughed. "You make it sound like a bad thing." I didn't look at her, didn't want to see the scrutinizing look I knew was on her face. Instead I watched the boat's purser coming down the pier carrying a canvas dead-letter packet.

"Think you'll come back?"

"Probably not." The sounds of the wharf diminished, the voice of the purser calling off names on his list a distant hum. I didn't understand this melancholy. I said, "Francine wouldn't be happy out here."

Bethany didn't say anything. She didn't have to. I knew what she thought of that.

I forced another laugh and tried to shrug off the uncomfortable silence between us. "You know as well as me this old river is going to roar out of its banks one of these days and wash this land clean of Bend City, and there goes your home."

She held me a moment in a thoughtful gaze before turning her pretty, green eyes away. "Home's not a place. Home's people. There're other towns. It doesn't take much to make a place a home if you've got someone to share it."

I envisioned Francine in her big house, standing as she often did in front of the tall hall mirror, her father in his smoky office bending over his ledgers, her mother scurrying here and there, always off to a tea or a civic meet. *Thomas Ragland.* Well, it would be different once we were married. Bethany was right. It wasn't the place, but the people. I felt a little better as we approached the pier. *Thomas Ragland!*

A tug on my sleeve brought me out of my thoughts. Bethany was giving me a curious look. She said, "Well?"

"Well what?"

"He's called your name twice now. Aren't you going to answer?"

"Final call for Thomas Ragland," the purser declared and then moved on. "Aaron Montgomery."

I stared at her. "Me?"

"You know anyone else named Thomas Ragland?"

"No one even knows I'm here."

"Better go make sure."

"Aaron Montgomery."

I pushed through the crowd and tapped the purser on the shoulder. He turned. "Mr. Montgomery?"

"Ragland. Thomas J."

"Ah." He fished about in his bag and pulled out a dog-eared envelope and peered at the name. "My, my, look at these postal stamps. Hardly can read your name past them all." He gave a short laugh. "I've never seen a letter addressed quite this way. I'm surprised the post office accepted it. It appears you've been on the move, and so has this letter. Here you go, sir." The purser scratched my name off his list and, giving a final call for Aaron Montgomery, moved on to the next name.

I recognized the hand at once. My sweet Francine! It was addressed to:

Mr. Thomas J. Ragland

General Delivery

Fort Rice, Dakota Territory, or someplace else.

Practically every square quarter inch of the envelope held a postal stamp or a scribbled note designating where it had ended up and where it was bound for. It'd followed me through a half-dozen towns and two or three Injun camps. The return address was mostly obliterated by the stamps and pencil scribbles, the name *Fra—Toutant* barely discernible.

I stared at the envelope in a sort of a daze, walking back to Bethany. I drew in a breath, realizing I hadn't done so in quite a while. My feelings were a-jumble. I was excited to have word from my beloved, yet worried something had gone terribly wrong back in St. Louis.

"Who's it from?" Bethany asked.

"Francine," I said. "This letter has been chasing me all across the territory."

"Are you going to open it, or just stand there gawking at it?"

With care, I ripped the edge of the envelope and pulled out a single sheet, folded in half. The stationery was pale purple.

Familiar. The page carried the Toutant monogram embossed at the top.

It began formally. *Dear Thomas.* My shoulders tightened, and my heart began to hammer. I'd always been *Tommy* to Francine. I think right then I knew what was going to follow, yet, hoping I was wrong, I plunged into the short missive.

Her words struck me like a hammer and broke me under their blows. I read it, not completely comprehending all of it.

"What does it say?" Bethany asked softly, seeing my reaction.

I couldn't speak past the knot in my throat. I gave the letter to her. When she finished reading it she looked up. "Who's Ford Fargo?"

Her voice seemed to come from some other world. My world had just crumbled away. I swallowed a couple times before words would come out. "I think he's the son of one of Pierre Toutant's business partners. An accountant, I think."

"She left you for a pencil pusher?"

I had no words. Bethany saw my feeble condition and said simply, "I'm sorry."

I nodded, unable to take it in, unable to think clearly, to know what it meant for me today . . . tomorrow . . . All I did know was that hunting down Chief suddenly didn't seem so urgent as it had just a handful of minutes ago.

Bethany didn't say a word, and for that I was grateful. Just her being there somehow made the wound Francine's letter had opened feel not quite so raw. Numbed, I felt myself fall into a cold fog as I turned my back on the steamer and started away. It wasn't until I'd crossed Bend Avenue and stopped in front of the boarded-up window of the Big Muddy Café that I realized Bethany was still at my side.

The cold fog lifted a little.

"What do I do now?" I said it more to myself than to her. I didn't expect her to have an answer. This was something I was going to have to work out, and it was going to take a good long time to do so.

"Bend City isn't a bad place," she said.

We started walking again. "The river'll wash it away."

"Maybe." Bethany went quiet again. A little way up the street, she paused to look into the window. I knew she wasn't really looking at the shoe display as she pretended to be. She spent a moment staring at her reflection in the glass and then tucked her hair in place here and there. I hadn't noticed her hair to be all that much out of place, but what do I know about women? At the moment it felt like not very much.

We moved on. A few paces farther and she said, "My mother had a full head of gray hair by the time she turned thirty."

"Oh?" I wasn't paying too much attention. The gray streaks in her hair weren't really fitting to my current misery.

She said, "I suspect I will, too."

I grunted something or other, not much concerned what color her hair was. But what she said next stopped me like a bullet from a buffalo gun.

"Mother went on to have another six children."

CHAPTER 26

It was the arrival of the package today that brought everything all to mind again.

Thinking back on it now, I was wrong about a couple things. Firstly, Old Mr. Missouri never did get angry enough to wash away Bend City. It took a fire to raze the building down by the wharf between River Street and Sawmill Road. Secondly, Beth had been right. Bend City wasn't all that bad a place after all.

Chief, Turk/Wert, and all the rest of it—that was four years ago. It took a good long while for me to come out of my slump over losing Francine, but, when I did, I had a new perspective on life. Beth and I married and moved into the Lemuels' abandoned house. We never did see Injun ghosts of any sort flying through the walls. A few months later we hitched Blue Shanks to a buggy and drove down to the US territorial marshal's office in Yankton to tend to Brian Bulger's appointment. Beth came back to Bend City a free woman, and, since no one else wanted the job, I came back wearing her badge. A year and three months later, Thomas Brian Ragland came into the world, and I strutted about town like a proud rooster handing out cigars.

Fire struck the wharf in '74. We were certain that was the end of the town, as no one was inclined to rebuild. Steamer traffic was still unreliable, and Bend City fared poorly for a while. More Injuns moved in, and more white men moved out. That all changed in '75, after the Custer expedition declared there to be gold in the Black Hills. News of gold spread across the country, and Bend City became a jumping off place for a new breed of "49ers" heading west to profane what were the Sioux's sacred mountains.

"Location, location," Wally Mace had once said.

The wharf got resurrected in stone and brick, levees were built, and a new pier twice as wide and half again as long as the old ones. Bend City expanded westward. McGill moved his stables uphill past the cemetery and grew wealthy selling pack animals to the flood of miners arriving daily. Beth and me, we took over Mace's empty hardware store, got rid of the shelves, built four more rooms, and renamed it Beth's Boarding House. With all the new arrivals, Beth was bringing in more money than I was marshaling.

One bright summer day, a shiny, black, gold-trimmed, chauffeur-driven Rockaway rolled into town, turning heads as it came up the street. It stopped on Bend Avenue right there in front of the old Big Muddy Café, which was now the Wong Tong Long Chinese laundry.

When the chauffeur opened the door, who stepped out of the carriage but Franklin and Margaret Collins! Franklin wore a tall, silk hat and a fine, gray, silk suit with a huge gold-nugget stickpin in the lapel. Margaret was dressed as a lady of fashion, with a parasol and a proper bustle. Franklin sought me out and pumped my hand until my shoulder ached. Apparently he'd discovered gold in a place called Dead Wood Gulch, and he said he owed it all to me. I felt flattered, and a little foolish when he told me those pebbles Bill Riley had flung at me had been gold nuggets!

Franklin and Margaret were heading down to Yankton to start a business called a *nursery*, an enterprise, I gathered, that grew trees and vegetables and such. I figured his new wealth had addled his brain. Who would ever buy such stuff? I seemed to recall Margaret Collins saying something along that line once upon a time ago.

But that wasn't the biggest surprise. The biggest surprise came this afternoon when a heavy package addressed to me was delivered to the boarding house. When I got home this evening Beth gave it to me, a confused look on her face. "I can't tell where it's from," she said.

The postal marks were in a foreign language, but the handwriting was English. I opened it, and when I drew out the letter, my jaw practically hit the tabletop. "It's from Chief!"

Beth leaned forward, her sparkling green eyes wide with sudden interest. "What does that thieving scoundrel have to say?"

So I read it aloud to her, the gist of it being that, after fleeing with the gold, jewels, Bill Riley, and Sherwin Turk, Chief collected $3,800 in bounty money. With his newfound wealth he headed east, ending up for a while in Chicago, where he happened to hear a street preacher by the name of Moody. Right there he got convicted of his sinful way of life, repented, and became determined to mend his fences. He traveled to Mirratavia and returned the gold and jewels, whereupon he was richly rewarded by a very thankful King Frederick, who soon after appointed Chief "minister of the court of exchequer" to the kingdom of Mirratavia. As if that wasn't enough, Chief convinced King Frederick to capitalize upon the realm's main source of wealth—its splendid Alpine mountain scenery and fresh air. For the last two years Chief had been hard at work, promoting Mirratavia as a tourist destination for wealthy Americans.

Stunned, Beth and I stared at each other in silence. Finally, Beth whispered, "Praise the Lord. What's in the box?"

That was the second surprise of the day. Inside the stout wooden box was a second box, a chest filled with gold mirramarks worth just about $3,800.

ABOUT THE AUTHOR

Douglas Hirt earned a bachelor's degree from the College of Santa Fe and a master of science degree from Eastern New Mexico University. During this time, he spent summers living in a tent in the New Mexico desert, conducting biological surveys for the US Department of Energy. Doug drew heavily from this desert life when writing his first novel, *Devil's Wind*. Doug's 1991 novel, *A Passage of Seasons,* won the Colorado Authors League Top Hands award. His books, *Brandish* and *Deadwood,* were 1998 and 1999 finalists for the SPUR award given by the Western Writers of America. *Bone Digger,* his 2015 novel, received the Peacemaker award from Western Fictioneers.

A short-story writer and author of forty books and numerous articles, Doug makes his home in Colorado with his wife, Kathy. They have two children and two grandchildren. When not writing or traveling, Doug enjoys restoring old English sports cars.

Learn more at www.DouglasHirt.com.

The employees of Five Star Publishing hope you have enjoyed this book.

Our Five Star novels explore little-known chapters from America's history, stories told from unique perspectives that will entertain a broad range of readers.

Other Five Star books are available at your local library, bookstore, all major book distributors, and directly from Five Star/Gale.

Connect with Five Star Publishing

Visit us on Facebook:
   https://www.facebook.com/FiveStarCengage

Email:
   FiveStar@cengage.com

For information about titles and placing orders:
   (800) 223-1244
   gale.orders@cengage.com

To share your comments, write to us:
   Five Star Publishing
   Attn: Publisher
   10 Water St., Suite 310
   Waterville, ME 04901